"I'd like a chance for us to start over."

"As friends?"

The corner of his mouth kicked up in a wry smile. "We were more than friends."

For one night, they'd been lovers. One night that had changed both of their lives more than Ryder could possibly know.

Lindsay swallowed. "Ryder, I—I can't. We can't go back. It's not possible."

"And what about going forward? Is that impossible, too?" Reading the answer in her gaze, he came to his own conclusion as he eased far away from her on the crowded bench. "Because you can't forgive me for what happened."

"It's not that," Lindsay protested quietly. "It's—"

That when I tell you the truth about what really happened that night, I don't know how you'll ever be able to forgive me.

THE PIRELLI BROTHERS:
These California boys know what love is all about!

Dear Reader,

High school... What memories do those four years hold for you? Some good...some bad. Maybe even the heartbreak of a first real crush.

For Lindsay Brookes, high school was a painful time. She longs to put her shy and awkward teenage days behind her, but Ryder Kincaid is the one boy she's never forgotten. The one boy she remembers every time she looks at her son.

When Lindsay returns to Clearville, she's not the same shy girl Ryder once knew, and he's not the same cocky captain of the football team. They've both changed over the past ten years, but can their high school reunion become a lasting relationship between two onetime sweethearts—or will secrets from the past tear them apart?

I hope you enjoy Lindsay and Ryder's journey toward love! Feel free to email me through my website, stacyconnelly.com, or at stacyconnelly@cox.net.

Happy reading!

Stacy Connelly

His Secret Son

Stacy Connelly

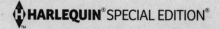 HARLEQUIN® SPECIAL EDITION®

Recycling programs
for this product may
not exist in your area.

ISBN-13: 978-0-373-65881-7

His Secret Son

Printed in U.S.A.

Stacy Connelly has dreamed of publishing books since she was a kid, writing stories about a girl and her horse. Eventually, boys made it onto the page as she discovered a love of romance and the promise of happily-ever-after. When she is not lost in the land of make-believe, Stacy lives in Arizona with her three spoiled dogs. She loves to hear from readers at stacyconnelly@cox.net or stacyconnelly.com.

Books by Stacy Connelly

Harlequin Special Edition

The Pirelli Brothers

Romancing the Rancher
Small-Town Cinderella
Daddy Says, "I Do!"
Darcy and the Single Dad
Her Fill-In Fiancé

Temporary Boss...Forever Husband
The Wedding She Always Wanted
Once Upon a Wedding
All She Wants for Christmas

Visit the Author Profile page at Harlequin.com for more titles.

To Cindy Kirk and Vicki Lewis Thompson—
Even though this book is set in the
fictional town of Clearville, California,
for me it will always be my "Tucson" book.

Chapter One

The place hadn't changed, Lindsay Brookes thought with a touch of nostalgia as she drove her SUV down Main Street. The tiny Northern California town where she'd been born and raised seemed caught in a time warp. The Victorian buildings that housed eclectic shops and restaurants had stood proudly for well over one hundred years, surviving the passage of time and even the occasional earthquake. Had she really thought they would undergo some sort of drastic modernization in the mere decade since she'd been gone?

Just because she'd worked so hard to make over the shy, awkward girl who'd graduated from Clearville High didn't mean the town had changed, too. Didn't mean the people who lived there would see how much she'd changed.

Shoving away the old insecurities, she sucked in a deep breath and tightened her hands on the wheel. She had her reasons for returning to her hometown, and the faster she accomplished her goals, the sooner she'd be back in

Phoenix, where she belonged. Where people only knew her as the strong, confident woman she was now and had no memory of the painfully shy, desperately lonely girl she'd once been.

As she glanced in the rearview mirror at one of her reasons for coming back, her heart filled with love—and yes, concern—at the sight of her son with his ever-present tablet in hand.

"Robbie? Robbie?"

"Huh?" He blinked as he looked up through his too-long blond bangs, his eyes slightly unfocused behind his Harry Potter–frame glasses.

It worried her a little, how fixated he was with his video games though she strictly limited them to ones she thought appropriate for a nine-year-old boy. She tried to monitor the time he spent playing them, too, but that was more of a challenge.

You were the same way at that age, she reminded herself even if it had been books and not games that had captured her imagination and led her away into the land of make-believe. But as much as she loved her son—his sweet shyness, his quirky humor, his sometimes scary intelligence—she didn't want him to follow so closely in her footsteps. She wanted him to have fun that didn't involve a high-definition screen and make friends who lived outside a computer-generated world.

"What do you want on your pizza?" she asked even though she already knew the answer.

"Pepperoni and peppers."

Lindsay didn't know where her son's craving for spicy foods came from. She could barely handle more than a few shakes of black pepper. Had to be from being born and raised in Phoenix, where Mexican restaurants dominated the landscape along with palm trees and cacti.

A sudden image teased the edges of her memory—a

brown-haired boy with laughing green eyes popping jalapeño slices into his mouth like candy—but she shoved the thought away. "Okay, pepperoni and peppers, but only on half, okay? You know Grandma Ellie and I don't like hot stuff."

Lindsay found a parking place on the street outside the pizza parlor and cut the engine. Lowering the visor, she took a moment to check her hair and makeup. Not that she expected a fashion disaster to have taken place during the fifteen-minute ride from her grandmother's house, but it never hurt to check.

Her honey-brown hair was still caught back in a clip at the nape of her neck despite Robbie's request to ride with the back window down and her daytime makeup—a soft brown eyeliner to highlight her blue-green eyes, mascara and a touch of lip gloss—was still in place. She took a moment to wipe a small smudge from the inside corner of one eye and tucked a stray curl behind her ear.

In her job working at a PR firm, she'd learned how much appearance mattered. And though she was on vacation, she saw no reason not to look her best. Especially when she never knew who she might run into…

Her stomach trembled at the thought, and she ran her suddenly damp palms down her beige slacks. As she climbed from the vehicle, the late-afternoon sunlight warmed her face and she took a moment to enjoy a cool breeze blowing in from the ocean.

The summer temperatures rarely rose above seventy, a refreshing change from the scorching heat they'd left behind. Back home, she'd already dug up all but the hardiest of flowers she'd planted during the mild winter and early spring, but here towering red and yellow snapdragons, purple petunias and snow-white alyssum flowed from brick planters. The green-and-white-striped awnings above the plate-glass windows waved in welcome, as did the open doors along the street—few of the buildings needing or even having the air-conditioning that was an absolute necessity living in the desert.

She wasn't alone in taking a moment to appreciate the gorgeous late-May day. Tourists strolled along the sidewalks and posed for pictures on benches outside the small shops. Families walked hand in hand—some heading toward the pizza parlor, others for the ice cream shop across the street. A group of laughing, roughhousing teenagers jostled by—all talking over each other in an almost indistinguishable babble—but Lindsay overheard one remark loud and clear.

"I can't believe we'll be starting college in three months!"

She did a quick double take at the trio. They all looked so young, sometimes it was hard for Lindsay to believe she'd ever been that age. Hard to believe that by the time she graduated, she'd already been—

"Oh, awesome! They have video games!" Robbie's voice cut into her thoughts.

As if he hadn't been playing a game the entire ride into town, she thought wryly.

Caught up in his excitement, he charged toward the restaurant doors.

"Robbie, wait! Watch—" Lindsay saw the accident waiting to happen but was too far away for her words to do any good as her son barreled into a man exiting the pizza joint. "—where you're going," she finished weakly, relieved when the man reached out to steady her reeling son with one hand without dropping the large pizza boxes balanced in his other.

"Whoa there, bud! No need to hurry. There's still plenty of pizza left inside."

No need to hurry.

The words—the voice—slammed into Lindsay's gut. She might have gasped, but the blow knocked the air from her lungs. Bright flashes of memory assaulted her, and she wanted to close her eyes, but she knew from too many sleepless nights that only made the images so much more intense.

"No need to hurry... We have all night."

So she steeled herself to face Ryder Kincaid for the first time in a decade—the familiar green eyes, rich brown hair, the sexy half smile that had stopped almost every girl's heart in high school—including her own. He'd always been undeniably gorgeous, even back then, and now... Lindsay swallowed. Now those good looks had been magnified by ten years' worth of distance, ten years' worth of maturity as he'd grown from a boy to a man.

That sexy smile was still there as he met her gaze. A dimple flashed, somewhat at odds with the five o'clock shadow defining the planes and angles of his sculpted cheekbones and rugged jawline. Her heart pounded as he stepped closer, the moment she'd at once dreaded and anticipated for all these years, finally at hand.

She'd pictured it a hundred times—his heartfelt apology for the way he'd treated her following that one warm spring night their senior year. Her cool dismissal as she proved once and for all how much better off she was without him.

How much better off *they* were without him.

But time, as it turned out, didn't change everything.

Not Ryder's smile or the casual nod he tipped in her direction before he walked by without a word.

And not Lindsay's shock as memories grabbed hold, dragging her back to the stupid, naive and *lonely* girl Ryder had used and tossed aside.

For a split second, the rich, tangy scent of pizza and whistles from the video games inside changed. Transformed into the slightly musty smell of a high school hallway and the peal of the morning bell from over a decade ago...

After years of silently, hopelessly loving Ryder Kincaid from a distance, she had finally, *finally* gotten noticed. More than noticed. So much more than noticed, and Lindsay had known her life would never be the same. She'd waited—heart pounding with excitement and anticipation—as she stood by his locker. A few fellow students glanced her way, as if wondering what *she* was doing in an area where the cool kids hung out, but she held her ground. Because soon everyone would know that she and Ryder Kincaid—*Ryder Kincaid*—were a couple.

She caught sight of him as he walked down the hallway, his hair falling over his forehead in a casual tousle, his green eyes laughing, his easy stride all loose-limbed confidence. He was surrounded by a group of friends, but then he'd always been so popular. Quarterback and captain of the football team, he had several scholarship offers. Everyone wanted Ryder.

Excitement soured into nervousness, but Lindsay pushed the feeling back. Everyone wanted Ryder, but he wanted *her*. Last Friday night had proved that. And so she waited for him to notice her, for his eyes to light up the way they had at Billy Cummings's party. Waited for him to pull her into his arms, to kiss her the way he had done only a few days ago. This time in front of all his friends so the whole high school would know that she was his girl...

Waited and watched in stunned, sickened disbelief as he walked right by her.

With a smile and a nod.

This isn't high school. This isn't high school. Lindsay repeated the words again and again. *You're not that same girl.*

Jerking her shoulders back, she held her head high as she marched toward the restaurant. She caught sight of Ryder's image in the large window as he strolled away, his broad shoulders, narrow hips and long denim-clad legs on display even in a wavy reflection. She watched as he jerked to a stop and slowly turned around. Saw the puzzled frown on his handsome face and thought maybe, just maybe, she heard him call out her name.

Lindsay kept going without breaking stride.

At least this time, she'd been the one to walk away.

Ryder Kincaid had known when he moved back to his hometown that he would have to eat more than a little crow.

Okay, so he had left town as the golden boy, the kid with the magical arm who'd taken their high school to the championship game and won it three out of four years. He'd been the captain of the football team, he'd been prom king and he'd dated the head cheerleader. He'd had scholarship offers from several colleges, and he'd chosen the biggest and best school to come knocking—even if that scholarship had only paid for part of his education.

After all, he'd been the big man on campus and all the best things in life were yet to come.

Big man on campus, he thought wryly. Big man in a small, small school in a small, small town.

He hadn't realized how small until he left. Until he spent his college career riding the bench—except for one magical fourth-quarter comeback he'd engineered his junior year—backup to a kid who'd gone on to be drafted by the NFL and was enjoying the professional career Ryder had only dreamed about.

Still, he'd made the most of his college years, taking part-time construction jobs to pay for all his scholarship didn't cover and earning a degree in architecture. He'd gone on to work at one of the most prestigious firms in San Francisco. A firm owned by his wife's—now ex-wife's—family. A job more than a few people around Clearville seemed to think he'd gotten on nepotism alone since the end of his marriage had also signaled the end of his career.

So, yeah, he'd had to grin and bear it when people jabbed him with the glory days of high school—*"Peaked too soon, didn't you, Kincaid?"*—and when they rubbed in the loss of his career—*"You know what they say, never a good idea to work for family"*—even though he really didn't think he deserved all that.

He'd had big dreams in high school—all centered on a game and a girl he loved. How did he end up the bad guy, the failure, when they had been the ones to betray him?

Ryder pushed aside the bitterness as he climbed the front steps to his brother's house. His family, at least, had welcomed him back with open arms, though they, too—or his mother at least—still looked at him with the question in her eyes. Where had it all gone wrong?

Marriage in the Kincaid family was supposed to be forever. His and Brittany's had barely made it to the six-year mark.

He balanced the pizzas in one hand, the hot crust warm even through a layer of cardboard, as he gave a quick knock and opened the front door. The sounds of kids playing—his nephews and whatever friends they might have invited over—rang out from the back of the house, and for an instant, Ryder thought of the boy at the pizza parlor. The one who'd barreled into him on his way out.

He'd gotten a quick glimpse of blond hair, glasses too big for a narrow face and a skinny body. After that, Ryder's attention had been claimed by the woman trailing behind.

After his marriage to Brittany and their turbulent on-again, off-again relationship spanning back to high school, Ryder had learned to keep his awareness when it came to the opposite sex well under wraps.

That didn't mean he didn't notice beautiful women. Hell, he was still a guy. And the woman who'd been standing on the sideway was definitely a beautiful woman. Her dark blond hair had been pulled back from her delicate features and wide blue-green gaze. At first glimpse, her eyes had widened with concern, then surprise as her warning to the boy died on her lips. Pale pink lips that had glistened with a hint of expertly applied makeup.

She hadn't had the look of a local picking up pizza for the family. Jeans and T-shirts were the typical dress code for almost every eating establishment in town, and her beige linen slacks and pale green blouse guaranteed she'd stand out—as if her beauty alone wasn't enough to set her apart from the crowd.

His instant attraction had caught him off guard. The ink on his divorce papers was barely dry, so even looking at another woman felt as smart as hitting himself in the head with a hammer. For the second time.

Only as he'd walked away did he realize that the woman looked familiar. Something in the not quite blue, not quite green of her eyes. In the expressive eyebrows a shade darker than her hair. In the heart-shaped contours of her face.

If the woman had indeed been Lindsay Brookes and if she'd ignored him as he'd called out her name, well, that was one smackdown he definitely deserved.

When he thought of the way he'd treated her after that one night their senior year, Ryder cringed. He tried hard *not* to think about the way he'd so pointedly dismissed her. He'd had his reasons at the time, good reasons, though Lindsay couldn't have known that. She couldn't have thought anything other than the obvious—that he'd slept with her on the rebound during another breakup with Brittany, used her and tossed her aside.

"Hey, why the frown?" his older brother, Bryce, asked as Ryder stepped into the kitchen. "Don't you know pizza's happy food?"

"It's…nothing really." He set the boxes on the granite island as he accepted the bottle of beer Bryce handed him with a nod of thanks. He couldn't help smiling as his brother moved around the kitchen with an ease that caught him a bit off guard.

Sure, all Bryce was doing was chopping a quick salad to add some veggies to their "guy night" dinner, but it was still strange to see him in his role as a dad. At times, when one of the boys called out "Dad," Ryder still expected his *own* father to be the one to answer, not his brother.

Though Ryder had tried to visit once or twice a year, getting together with Bryce's family over the holidays or taking a trip over summer break to Disneyland hadn't clued him in to how hands-on his brother was in his day-to-day dad duties. Since moving back the previous fall, Ryder had gotten a real chance to see Bryce, and his wife, Nina, in action.

The couple worked well together, their conversation filled with lighthearted teasing, respect and a love that had stabbed him with a sense of envy—even before his divorce.

"Do you remember Lindsay Brookes?" he asked. "She was in my grade in school."

"Think so. Real bookworm, right? Kind of a know-it-all?" Bryce asked as he made quick work chopping a green pepper.

"Yeah, but she wasn't like that. Not really."

"I don't recall the two of you being friends back then."

"She helped me out our senior year." He'd always prided himself on getting decent grades, despite his jock status, but that year he'd done more partying than studying and his test scores had started to reflect that. "She tutored me in calculus."

"Sounds like a brain to me."

"Oh, yeah, she was supersmart." Ryder gave a short laugh. "And she couldn't seem to stop herself from pointing out when someone made a mistake. She thought she was being helpful. She never seemed to get that the other kids didn't see it that way."

"Right after graduation…she surprised everybody when she started hanging out with that Pirelli cousin, right?" Bryce asked over his shoulder as he opened the fridge and pulled out a small carton of tomatoes.

"Yeah, I guess they'd gotten to be friends over the years when he came to town to visit his family, but then that summer…" Everyone else might have been surprised to see the shy, quiet girl hook up with the brooding Tony Pirelli, but all Ryder had felt was relief. He couldn't have broken her heart too badly if she'd immediately fallen for another guy. Lindsay and Tony had been inseparable that summer.

"I don't know what a hunk like that sees in a book-brain like her," Brittany had scoffed when the two couples ran into each other at the Fourth of July picnic in the town square.

Ryder had made some sound of agreement, but he'd known then that he'd done the best thing—if not the right thing—in breaking things off with Lindsay. Though he and Brittany had broken up during that brief period when he slept with Lindsay, his girlfriend would have made Lindsay's life a living hell had she found out about the two of them.

"That's right. And then—" Bryce cut off, and he made a face as he put down the knife. "When did we turn into a couple of women gossiping in the kitchen?"

"Probably about the same time you put on that apron," Ryder said with a tip of his beer bottle in his brother's direction.

Bryce looked down before defensively saying, "Hey, these tomatoes are juicy."

Ryder's grin faded away as he thought of what his brother hadn't said.

And then Lindsay got pregnant.

He and Brittany had already moved into their dorms by then, but the Clearville grapevine traveled long-distance. When he first heard the news, for a panicked, "what the hell am I going to do?" moment, he'd wondered even as his brain rejected the very idea.

Couldn't be mine.

It was just one time.

We used protection.

No way. There's no way...

And then Brittany had quickly filled him in on the details—how everyone knew Tony Pirelli was the father, how his family was in an uproar because Tony refused to marry Lindsay, how Lindsay's family had left town in disgrace. All of it as juicy as Bryce's vine-ripe tomatoes.

"Why the trip down memory lane anyway?"

"I heard she's in town for a few weeks to help out her grandmother, and I thought I might have seen her when I was picking up the pizzas. She looked...good."

"Her grandmother?" Bryce asked, an incredulous note filling his voice.

"No, not—" Ryder caught sight of the smirk his brother was trying to hide a split second too late and tossed a nearby towel into Bryce's grinning face. "Very funny."

Catching the towel with ease, he draped it over one shoulder. "I'd say Lindsay'd have to look spectacular to catch your eye. Haven't you sworn off all women since the divorce?"

"I didn't mean it like that." Although the hell of it was, Lindsay *had* looked spectacular. But more than that, she'd had an air of confidence, of success. A woman who'd found her place out in the big wide world and a far cry from the girl who'd struggled to fit in at tiny Clearville High. "I was glad to see that she's doing well."

In a small way, it eased the burden of that old guilt he'd been carrying around. Sure, he'd been a stupid, horny teenager, but that was no excuse for treating Lindsay the way he had. He owed her an apology and an explanation at the least and, maybe if he was lucky, a way to make up for his behavior at best.

Thanks to the phone call he'd received earlier that day, he knew he'd get his chance soon enough.

Chapter Two

She'd survived.

Her first run-in with Ryder Kincaid on only her second day back in town, and she'd survived.

Lindsay blew out a breath, still more shaken by the split-second encounter than she liked to admit. Ten years. Ten years! She was supposed to be over him. She *was* over him. Just not quite over the shock of seeing him, that was all.

Glancing around the pizza parlor play area, she felt her heartbeat settling as her gaze landed on Robbie. She'd quickly agreed to his request to play the video games while they waited for their order. She needed a moment to herself, and she'd hoped he might have a chance to talk with some of the other kids racing between newer video games and older throwbacks from when she was a kid—foosball, air hockey, even a tiny basketball hoop and net. But Robbie had locked in on conquering alien invaders and had barely done more than lift a skinny shoulder in a half-hearted shrug when one of the other boys stopped to talk to him. Within a few seconds, the boy wandered off and Robbie hunkered down over the joystick, his bangs falling over the frames of his glasses.

Her heart ached for her son. For the all-too-familiar shyness that made something inside him shut down when he tried to talk to kids his own age. Lindsay remembered the feeling so well. The fear, the panic of doing the wrong thing, saying the wrong thing. And the self-consciousness that made it seem that no matter what she did or what she said, it was always wrong.

She knew she couldn't expect too much. She and Robbie would be in town for a few weeks—just long enough for her to convince her grandmother that it was time to sell the house and move to Phoenix to be closer to Lindsay and her parents. But during that short time, she hoped Robbie would find some kids to hang out with. Clearville was a tourist town, always filled with summer visitors— most of them families with children. It would do him so much good to make new friends, and maybe the short time frame would help him be more open to the possibility. It was something she'd encouraged on the trip up from Phoenix, not that her suggestion was well received.

"I already have a best friend," Robbie had insisted stubbornly.

"I know, but would it be so bad to meet some new friends?" she'd asked, careful not to bring up the reminder that his best friend had recently moved across the country.

Scott Wilcott and his family had been their next-door neighbors for the past three years—a lifetime for little boys. The two had bonded instantly, and Lindsay had been so grateful, not only for Robbie's friendship with Scott, but also for the time her son got to spend with Scott's father. She knew how important it was for her son to have a male role model in his life. Gary Wilcott had helped fill that void by including Robbie in their family outings and making the boy feel as welcome in their home as he was in his own.

With the Wilcotts moving away, Lindsay worried as much about Robbie missing Gary as she did about him missing Scott.

"Lindsay? Lindsay Brookes?"

Starting at the sound of her name being called out amid kids laughing and bells and whistling going off in the gaming area, she turned in the small booth to see a short, curvy blonde woman heading in her direction.

"Cherrie... Been a long time, hasn't it?"

"Ten years!" the other woman agreed.

And yet not nearly long enough, Lindsay thought as she kept her smile firmly locked in place. Along with Brittany Baines, Cherrie Macintosh and a handful of other girls had ruled the school back in the day. The popular kids who could make life hell for anyone not in their small circle. As a shy bookworm, Lindsay had mostly escaped their noticed.

Mostly.

"Did you hear Lindsay Brookes got herself knocked up?"

"I'd have thought that girl would die a virgin!"

"They always say it's the quiet ones who surprise you."

"She must have done it on purpose to trap Tony Pirelli."

"Well, it's not like a guy that hot is hanging out with her for her brain!"

"Goodness," Cherrie remarked, "if I hadn't heard you were coming to town, I don't think I would have even recognized you. I mean, you were such a mousy little thing back then, weren't you?"

Yes, she had been. But that was a long time ago, and she wasn't that girl anymore. She had five years under her belt working for a high-profile PR firm in Phoenix. She could put on a smile and spin the truth with the best of them. Reminding herself of that, she slid from the booth.

In high school, she'd hated her above-average height. Hated anything that might make her stand out in a crowd, and she'd spent most of those years hunched over—even when her nose wasn't buried in a book. But she'd learned— heck, studies proved—that tall people were often seen as smarter and more successful than people of a lesser stature. And even in low-heeled sandals she'd chosen to wear to run for pizza, she towered over Cherrie. "You're right. I was. Thank goodness we aren't all still the people we were back in high school."

Cherrie blinked as if trying to figure out the subtle dig behind Lindsay's words. "Oh, sure. I mean, that was, like, forever ago, right?"

Was it Lindsay's imagination or had a hopeful note entered the other woman's voice? As if Lindsay might have forgotten the cruel gossip that had shadowed her those last weeks before she and her parents left town.

Without Brittany and the rest of the squad around her, Cherrie didn't look all that intimidating. If anything, she appeared a bit needy and eager to please. Someone who would have gone along with the other kids as a way to fit in.

Lindsay wouldn't have expected to feel sorry for anyone in that old group from high school, but maybe that also proved how much she had changed. "You're right. All water under the bridge now."

"Yeah, sure. It is. And it will be great to catch up with everyone at the reunion next month. You'll still be here then, won't you?"

Lindsay could think of few things she wanted to do less than attending her ten-year reunion. Reminiscing over four years of pure hell? Yeah, that sounded fun. "I'm not sure if I'll make it or not," she said to Cherrie.

"Oh, well…" The other woman gave a small laugh. "It's funny, though, if you'd been here a few seconds earlier, we could have had our own minireunion. You just missed seeing Ryder Kincaid. You know he's moved back, right?"

"I'd heard something about that." Under the bridge or not, Lindsay wasn't about to churn up that water by admitting to Cherrie—who still seemed to enjoy spreading a bit of gossip—that Ryder's presence had prompted her own return to their hometown.

Leaning forward, Cherrie said, "He left Brittany, you know. Out of the blue. Total surprise. Brittany and I, we're still, like, best friends, though we don't see each other much. I had hoped she'd come back for the reunion, but she said it would be too hard. All those memories of her and Ryder together, you know? She's trying to be strong, but you can tell she's devastated."

"Well, I'm sorry to hear that," Lindsay said, the words not entirely untrue even if her concern wasn't so much for Brittany.

"I mean, they were together *forever*," Cherrie stressed, "the perfect couple and the marriage everyone thought would last!" Lowering her voice a bit more, she added, "Ryder's not talking, but what can he say? To just walk away like he did…"

The buzz of her words blended in with the laugher and sirens from the play area. What did Lindsay really know about Ryder? In all truthfulness—despite what her teenage heart had believed back then—she'd hardly known him as a boy. She didn't have any idea what kind of man he was now. What kind of father he might be…

When she heard about his divorce and that he'd moved back to Clearville, Lindsay had taken it as a sign—after a decade of secrets, half-truths and out-and-out lies—it was time to come clean. But this couldn't be simply about doing the right thing. Telling the truth had to be about doing the *best* thing for Robbie. Her son mattered most, more than the guilt she'd carried for so long, more than Ryder's rights as a father. Robbie came first.

Every story had two sides, and while Brittany's still-best friend, Cherrie, would know Brittany's side, Lindsay needed to hear Ryder's. She needed to know the kind of man she was letting into her son's life. Needed to know that he wouldn't turn his back on her son the way he apparently had done on his wife and marriage.

Lindsay swallowed hard even as nerves swirled through her stomach. After more than a decade of loving and at times hating Ryder Kincaid from afar, it was time to get up close and personal.

"Now, there's the granddaughter I know and love! I was wondering when she might show up."

Lindsay rolled her eyes at her grandmother Ellie's teasing as she stepped into the kitchen and self-consciously ducked her head. She pushed her heavy glasses farther up her nose, wishing she'd had time to shower and do her hair and makeup, not to mention put in her contacts before coming down for breakfast.

Back home, Robbie would fix himself a bowl of cereal and some fruit during the week and was content to play video games or watch television on the weekends, giving Lindsay the time she needed to get ready in the morning. But as she'd learned on her first day, Ellie didn't believe cold cereal and a banana was an adequate meal for a growing boy.

By the time Lindsay came down, her grandmother had fixed a spread worthy of an all-you-can-eat breakfast buffet. And while Ellie insisted she loved to cook, Lindsay was there to help take care of her grandmother, not to be taken care of.

So on this morning, as soon as she heard sounds coming from the kitchen, she'd hurried from the bedroom after doing no more than brushing her teeth and putting on the glasses she needed to keep from killing herself on the way down the stairs. She smiled wryly as she saw the vast ingredients her grandmother had already compiled in that short amount of time.

Flour, eggs, sugar and blueberries for homemade pancakes, potatoes for hash browns, a thick slab of presliced bacon, a kettle of fragrant chamomile tea already brewing on the stove and in the middle of it all, her grandmother. Ellie Brookes was a tiny woman with the type of petite build Lindsay had always envied. Her silver-streaked blond hair was pulled back into a short ponytail at the nape of her neck and she wore a ruffled apron over her beige capris and pale blue T-shirt.

Anyone who mistook her grandmother's small stature as a sign of fragility would quickly change their minds when they witnessed her sharp wit disguised behind a sweet smile on her round, slightly lined face.

"This isn't the real me, Gran," Lindsay said with a glance down at the pink pajama bottoms decorated with shoes and a matching T-shirt that read If the Shoe Fits, Buy It! "Not anymore."

"Of course it is, dear. You're hiding the real you behind those fancy clothes of yours, same way you used to hide behind all those books back in high school."

Lindsay's jaw dropped a little even as she stepped up to the worn Formica counter and reached for the loaf of bread. "That's not— Those fancy clothes as you call them *are* the real me. I'm a professional now. I have an image to maintain. It's an important part of my job."

A job that was still hers—at least for now. With the PR firm going through a buyout by their main competitor, she'd heard plenty of rumors that no one was safe.

"An image," her grandmother murmured beneath her

breath as she expertly cracked eggs into the mixing bowl. "You are more than an image."

"I'm not saying that's all I am. Only that—"

"It's all you allow people to see," Ellie interrupted before flipping on the mixer to punctuate her statement and have the last word.

Lindsay shook her head at her grandmother's undeniable hardheadedness. Had she really thought this would be easy? she asked herself as she bent toward the lower cabinets for a skillet. She pulled at the cupboard door once, then again and almost lost her balance and tumbled backward when it finally gave way.

"Careful, dear," Ellie called out over the high-pitched whirl of the mixer. "That door sticks."

"So I noticed," Lindsay muttered but not so loudly that her grandmother could hear. She'd also noticed the uneven brick path out front, the sagging porch steps, the crooked outlets, the cracking grout on the bathroom floors. She shuddered slightly to think of all she couldn't see. What about the wiring, the plumbing, the actual structure holding up the charming but aging Victorian?

With such an old house, maintenance was a full-time job—one her grandfather had gladly taken on after retiring from the local post office. But while Robert Brookes had been a wonderful man, loving husband, doting father and grandfather, a handyman he was not. As his various attempts proved to Lindsay's untrained eye.

Her parents had warned her that the house would need serious work before they could put it on the market, and she had to tread carefully—both about the quality of the work Ellie's late husband had done and about selling the house Ellie loved.

Her grandmother was far too smart not to have figured out the reason behind Lindsay's visit, once the phone calls from Lindsay and her parents failed to do the trick. So far,

Ellie had changed the subject anytime Lindsay so much as discussed all the benefits of moving to Phoenix. Even the best, most convincing argument Lindsay could think of—"you'll get to see more of me and Robbie"—had been met with Ellie's patented smile.

"Something I could do right here if you and my great-grandson would move back home."

Stubborn, Lindsay thought with a sigh. But so was she.

"Just needs a bit of elbow grease," Ellie said, and for a split second, Lindsay thought her grandmother was talking about what might be needed to get her to move from the home she loved.

Still, Lindsay grabbed at the opening while she could. "You're right, Gran. A little bit of elbow grease and some TLC. I know it's been hard for you to keep up with everything since Granddad died," she added gently.

Ellie sighed as she shut off the mixer. "Your grandfather loved puttering around the place. He was always happier when he had a project to work on."

"Like you're always happier when you have someone to cook for," Lindsay said as she reached out to set the skillet on the stove and steal a handful of blueberries on the way back.

"Those are for the pancakes," Ellie scolded as Lindsay knew she would. "And you're right. Upkeep on this place was your grandfather's love, not mine."

Lindsay carefully swallowed the juicy bite-size fruit, almost afraid of ruining the moment. Was her grandmother starting to see things her way? "It's a big house, Gran. A lot of work for one person."

Ellie nodded as she wiped her hands on her apron. "That's why I've made a decision."

Pinpricks of tears stung Lindsay's eyes. How hard it must be for her grandmother to realize she couldn't stay in her own house. The place where she'd lived with her husband and young children. The place where she'd raised her family, grown old and said goodbye to the man she loved after over fifty years of marriage.

A pang hit her chest as Lindsay admitted she, too, would miss the old house where she'd spent some of the best parts of her childhood. She loved her parents, of course, but going to Grandma and Grandpa's had always been such a treat.

But a house was just a house, and once Ellie moved to Phoenix, their family would see each other far more often. "It's the right thing to do, Gran."

"Oh, I know. It's time," Ellie said, her voice cheerier than Lindsay might have expected. But then again, once Ellie made up her mind, there was no going back.

The ringing of the doorbell interrupted before Lindsay could get too emotional, and she quickly blinked back tears as her grandmother turned toward the sound. "Can you watch these pancakes while I get that?" Ellie asked, already stripping off her apron and passing the spatula to Lindsay.

She could hear the low sound of voices—her gran's familiar sweet tones and a lower, undeniably masculine murmur—as she watched the pancakes, waiting for the bubbles to rise to the top.

She'd flipped the first, somewhat successfully, when the voices grew louder. Her grandmother wasn't— Oh, yes, she was. Ellie was leading whoever was at the door straight to the kitchen.

Lindsay didn't need to look around to know there was no escape. She was still in her pajamas, for goodness' sake! She didn't even want to think about her hair or her glasses.

Panic started to build despite the deep breaths she took. *I don't want anyone to see me like this. This isn't me anymore!*

Bookworm Brookes—the geekiest girl at Clearville High. But it was too late to do anything but grin and fake it.

To put the best spin possible on the situation. A situation that grew so much worse as her grandmother stepped into the kitchen with a smile...and Ryder Kincaid following on her heels.

A nightmare, Lindsay thought. It had to be. Like the ones where you were naked in front of a crowd. But instead of naked, she was in her cartoon pajamas and thick-framed glasses. Which, as she met Ryder's amused grin, was almost worse.

"Lindsay, dear, you remember Ryder Kincaid, don't you?" Ellie asked as she slid the spatula from Lindsay's nerveless fingers and took over at the stove.

"I, um, yes. I remember." And though there was nothing remotely suggestive in her voice or in the moment, Lindsay swallowed as her gaze locked with Ryder's. In an overwhelming, soul-stealing rush, she remembered... everything.

She'd been so nervous and yet so eager when Ryder kissed her that first time. Her heart had pounded so hard she was half-afraid it was going to leap right out of her chest. Every kiss, every touch had felt like magic, and she'd known her life would never be the same...

And oh, hadn't she been right about that even if she'd been so wrong about *everything* else?

"Hey, Lindsay." Was it her imagination or did Ryder's voice sound a little deeper, a little rougher around the edges, as if he, too, was suffering from some flashbacks of his own? "Good to see you again."

Her stomach twisting into knots, she asked, "What... what are you doing here, Ryder?"

His familiar grin was back, and Lindsay resisted the urge to slap herself. Hadn't he proved time and again that that night had meant nothing to him? He'd hardly spoken to her in the weeks that followed, striding through the high school halls with Brittany Baines on his arm. Prom king and queen, the school's golden couple. He'd forgotten all about her in the time it took to drop her back on her front porch and drive away.

"Your gran invited me."

"What? Why?" For a split second, the room spun as her world tilted. Her grandmother couldn't possibly know—no one knew about her and Ryder. No one except for Tony Pirelli, the boy—man now, though Lindsay hadn't seen him since the summer after she graduated—whom everyone believed to be Robbie's father. And even then, Lindsay hadn't mentioned Ryder's name when she confessed her terrifying secret.

Only that she'd been so, so stupid and was so, so scared...

"I don't know what to do, Tony. I can't tell the father. I just...can't."

"So don't."

"What?"

"Don't say anything. Anyone asks about the father, tell 'em it's none of their business."

"But you know people will think—"

"People can think whatever the hell they want. The trick is learning not to give a damn."

It was a trick Tony Pirelli could give lessons in. He'd already angered his parents, first by dropping out of college midway through his second semester and more recently with his intention to join the marines.

"But what...what will you tell your family?"

He'd grinned at her—his typical indolent, almost insolent smile. *"That's easy. I'll tell 'em the last thing they'd ever believe."*

"What's that?"

"The truth."

His plan had worked. The more he protested his innocence and hotly denied responsibility, the guiltier he sounded. Before long, everyone accepted he was the father of her baby—including his family. And for all these years, for the sake of their friendship, Tony had carried the weight of their disappointment so that she could keep the true identity of Robbie's father a secret.

"Didn't you know, Lindsay?" Ellie was asking. "Ryder moved back last year."

"Yes, I'd heard. But that doesn't exactly explain why you invited him over for breakfast," Lindsay answered back in an aside that must have been loud enough for Ryder to hear, judging by the way one side of his mouth kicked up.

Ellie laughed. "I didn't invite him for breakfast—though you're welcome to join us," she called over her shoulder to the man in question.

"Love to."

Of course he would, Lindsay thought as she drew in a breath. Nightmare. Really, really had to be a nightmare. "Then why did you invite him over, Gran?" she asked even as habit kicked in and she reached for the plates to set the table.

"To take a look at fixing up the house. Isn't that what you and your parents have been trying to get me to do for months now?" Ellie's expression seemed a shade too innocent, but Lindsay was too caught off guard by her words to focus on the meaning behind them.

"But Ryder—" Her protest died on her lips as she realized she didn't know exactly what Ryder had been doing for a living since he returned home. He'd worked at his in-laws' firm in San Francisco, building billion-dollar, award-winning high-rises. Not something there was much need for in Clearville.

Still… "You're…you're a handyman?" Lindsay asked as she carried the plates toward the eat-in nook.

A very small nook she couldn't get to without stepping way too close to Ryder. She tried to squeeze by, but he moved directly into her path and reached for the plates. "I do like to consider myself handy."

Lindsay didn't want to remember all the places those skilled hands had once touched while standing in her grandmother's kitchen. Didn't want to remember—ever. But she did. She remembered every touch, every kiss, every mistaken belief that what she was feeling—what they were both feeling—had to be love.

And that Ryder seemed to want her to remember was just…cruel. Like tossing her foolishness for falling for him, for thinking making love with him meant something, back in her face.

The stoneware plates, still caught between both their hands, rattled as her hands shook. "Hey, Lindsay," Ryder said softly, his eyebrows pulling low. But whatever else he might have said was lost by the thump of footsteps coming down the stairs.

"Mom, what's—"

Robbie's typical question of "what's to eat?" cut off as the boy slid to a stop in the kitchen doorway, his gaze shifting between his mother and Ryder. Lindsay jerked back so quickly only Ryder's fast reflexes saved the plates from crashing to the tile floor.

"Hey, honey." Reaching out, she restrained herself from pulling him into her embrace. Instead she took small comfort in resting a hand on her son's narrow shoulder. He wasn't big on hugs anymore, at least not when other people were around. And she no longer had the power to kiss an owie and make the hurt go away. It was all part of growing up, she knew. Part of changing from boy to man, a transition she knew nothing about.

And seeing the two of them—father and son standing side by side for the first time—she felt a wave of dizziness rock her. Her heartbeat pounded in her ears, drowning out all other sounds and blurring the edges of her vision until she could see nothing else but her boy and the man in front of her.

Everyone had always told her how much Robbie took after her. But then again, everyone also thought dark-haired, dark-eyed Tony Pirelli was her son's father, and he and Robbie looked nothing alike. So little wonder people saw the resemblance between mother and son in their dark blond, wavy hair, blue-green eyes and slender builds. It was all Lindsay ever saw—until now.

But now, with Robbie and Ryder together, wasn't there a similarity in the shape of their chins, their wide foreheads, the arch of their eyebrows? Even, heaven help her, the cowlick at the part of their hair, far more noticeable in Ryder's short style than in her son's too-long bangs.

Not a mirror image by any means. More of a time progression of what Robbie might look like in another twenty years…

"Who's that?" Robbie murmured, his head lowered so far he might have been asking the question of the racecar speeding across the front of his shirt.

"Robbie, this is…"

Your father.

Chapter Three

For that split second, Lindsay nearly blurted out the truth she had kept secret for so long. The promised relief from the weight that had settled in her chest from the time Robbie was a toddler and started calling her own father "Dada" was almost overwhelming. But this couldn't be about her. She had to think about her son…and about Ryder and the kind of father he might make.

She had no idea how Ryder would react to the news. He could turn his back on Robbie the same way he'd turned his back on her. Or—and wasn't this her greater fear?—he could try to take Robbie away. He had nine years' worth of visitation rights. Lump that altogether and he could steal the boy she loved more than her own life away from her for a long, long time. Not that joint custody worked that way, but the words *joint custody* filled her with a fear no amount of truth telling could free her from.

No, she had to get to know Ryder much better than she

did now—much better than she'd even known him in high school—before she would tell him about Robbie.

So she said, "Robbie, this is Ryder Kincaid."

"Hey, bud," Ryder said, sticking his hand out. He had his fist closed and Robbie somewhat cautiously reached out to bump knuckles. His arm skinny, pale and still little-boy smooth; Ryder's well-muscled, tanned and covered with a light sprinkling of masculine hair. His tone more relaxed than Lindsay would have expected, he added, "Your mom and I used to be friends back in school."

"Really?" Robbie glanced sidelong from behind his glasses at Lindsay as if waiting for her to verify a truth he couldn't quite believe.

Yeah, well, she'd always known her son was smart. Smarter than her teenage self, who'd actually believed she and Ryder had something more than friendship.

Still, she faked a smile and agreed, "That's right. We started hanging out while I was tutoring Ryder in math."

It was a bit of a low blow. Robbie had never needed any kind of help in school—not from her and certainly not from another student. Pointing out that Ryder had was more than a little immature.

But Ryder merely grinned. "That's right. Your mom was the smartest girl I knew."

Not smart enough to keep from being totally fooled by him. But Lindsay swallowed her anger the same way she had a decade ago—by focusing on Robbie. "Why don't you finish setting the table?" she suggested with a nod at the stack of plates Ryder had already placed on the table.

"Set it for four, sweetie," her grandmother called out from her place at the stove, proving she'd been listening in all along. "Mr. Kincaid is joining us for breakfast."

Ryder grinned at Robbie. "Call me Ryder. Mr. Kincaid is my dad."

The boy muttered something beneath his breath that

might have been Ryder's name, but Lindsay could barely hear over the words echoing through her head.

"Mr. Kincaid is my dad."

But with Robbie gathering silverware from the kitchen drawer and her grandmother flipping the bacon popping in the skillet, Lindsay took the opportunity to ask, "What are you doing here, Ryder?"

"Like your gran said. She called looking for a quote to fix up the house. You don't have a problem with that, do you?"

He lifted his eyebrows in challenge, bringing back the memories of the dares she hadn't had the will to resist. Yes, she'd tutored him in calculus, and yes, Ryder had gone on to pass the class. But more often than not, he'd convince her to slip away from the library and sneak off to the square or the rocky, secluded beach not far from town.

It hadn't been much of a risk, really, as they'd never done anything more than sit on a shady park bench or walk on the beach and talk. So perfectly harmless if she didn't count falling headlong in love with him.

And while Lindsay wanted to believe she'd outgrown such foolishness, this was one challenge she couldn't refuse. She didn't dare admit she had a problem with Ryder taking a look at the house—not without giving him cause to wonder why. And hadn't she been looking for a way to get to know him? A better opportunity wasn't likely to fall in her lap, and yet—

I don't want him here. Not so close to Robbie. Not where their every move would be under her grandmother's watchful eye...

"I don't suppose it would hurt to get a quote," she said finally. "But I'm going to need references."

"Of course," he agreed with mock seriousness. "You wouldn't be the girl I remember if you didn't do your homework first."

"The girl you remember," she muttered beneath her breath with a sarcastic scoff. "Right."

She turned to head back to the kitchen, but Ryder caught her arm. Lindsay nearly gasped at the unexpected contact even though it was nothing more than a split second before he let go. Had he sensed her reaction? Or make that *over*-reaction? She didn't dare look him in the face. Good Lord, could this morning get any more humiliating?

"I'm sorry about yesterday. Seriously, Lindsay, when I first saw you…I didn't recognize you. You looked so different."

Because she'd changed, she reminded herself. And not only on the outside. She was a new person. A stronger, smarter, more confident person. So she forced herself to meet his gaze.

Sincerity filled his expression as he said, "I didn't realize it was you." A faint smile curved his lips. "Seeing you today, I'd have recognized you in a heartbeat."

And then that mossy gaze traveled from her sleep-tousled hair caught back in its mousy ponytail, her thick glasses and makeup-free face, down her cutesy and by no means sexy pajamas, all the way down to her feet. Heat rose over her skin every inch of the way.

Embarrassment. Pure and simple embarrassment.

"Gotta tell you, I'm digging the doggie slippers."

Lindsay glanced down, and two pairs of googly eyes stared back up at her. The beagle slippers Robbie had given her for her birthday as a not so subtle reminder of the dog he wanted.

I really need to wake up before this nightmare gets any worse.

Muttering an excuse about helping her grandmother, Lindsay ducked away. When no convenient hole opened up to swallow her, she joined her grandmother at the stove and reached for the plate of hash browns. "You could have warned me you'd invited someone over this morning."

"I'm sorry, sweetie. But really, I thought you'd be happy. Isn't this what you and your parents have wanted?"

Lindsay exhaled as she reminded herself that this wasn't only about her. Her grandmother had made a tough decision about selling the house, and if getting the repairs over and done with made things easier on Ellie, then Lindsay could certainly give her gran a break. "You're right, of course. And I am glad. It's for the best, you'll see."

"Oh, I have no doubt. Just think, once the repairs are made and everything's back in shape, I'll have no reason not to stay right where I am."

With a satisfied smile, Ellie grabbed the platter loaded down with pancakes, crispy bacon and scrambled eggs and turned toward the eat-in nook. "Now, who's hungry?"

Robbie and Ryder both called out, but Lindsay's own appetite disappeared as her stomach dropped. *Stay in the house?* So much for convincing her grandmother to sell. Instead she'd given Ellie reason to dig in her heels even further.

Looking over at the table in time to see Ryder cajole a laugh out of her typically shy son over spearing the same piece of bacon with their forks, Lindsay swallowed her own, slightly hysterical laughter as she tried to figure out how everything had slipped so far from her control.

In San Francisco, client breakfasts were held in towering high-rises with multimillion-dollar views overlooking the bay. Often those meetings were catered by some of the best restaurants around, but Ryder could honestly say the food couldn't compare with the simple, home-cooked dishes Lindsay's grandmother prepared. The bacon was exactly how he liked it—crisp but not too crisp—and the

pancakes so light and fluffy and flavorful he'd waved aside
Ellie's offer of maple syrup.

If this was a typical breakfast in the Brookes' house-
hold, well, he'd be tempted to stop by every morning.

And not just for the food...

Ryder wanted to ignore the sly voice that sounded far
too much like his big brother's, but he couldn't stop his
gaze from sliding toward Lindsay, seated diagonally across
the table from him.

Her appearance was a far cry from the sophisticated
woman he'd seen the day before. Her pajamas were sleep-
rumpled, her tousled hair caught up in a crooked ponytail, her face free of even a hint of makeup. Ryder had no
doubt she was more than a little embarrassed, but all he
could think was how fresh-faced and natural she looked.
How real...

And after life with Brittany, the masks she wore and
the games she played, *nothing* was more appealing than a
woman with nothing to hide.

He had to swallow a smile every time Lindsay self-
consciously adjusted the glasses she hadn't worn the day
before. She'd clearly switched to contacts and was uncomfortable in the thick tortoiseshell frames that seemed
too big for her delicate features. But the more she messed
with the glasses, the more he noticed them, and the more
he had to fight that smile.

Ryder still wasn't sure what it was that had drawn him
to her when they were teenagers. To say they didn't run
in the same circles was an understatement. He'd spent
his days in the limelight, surrounded by kids in the cool
crowd, while Lindsay blended into the shadows. It wasn't
that the other kids disliked her. More that no one really
got the chance to know her. He couldn't count how many
times he'd smiled or said hi to her in the halls, but she'd
duck her head and all but run away.

Just as she had earlier that morning.

But this Lindsay, the grown-up Lindsay—despite the throwback glasses, cartoon pajamas and fuzzy dog slippers—was stronger than the girl he remembered. She could have disappeared into one of the bedrooms upstairs.

Instead she'd taken her place at the table, but her nerves still showed in her rigid posture. Her gaze kept cutting over to her son every few seconds, though Ryder wasn't sure what she expected the boy to do. The kid—Robbie, wasn't it?—was far more reserved than his nephews, who'd talk anyone's ear off. Maybe it was being an only child. During his own childhood with his older brother and younger sister, there was always someone to talk to, talk over or argue with. Meals were always a noisy, rambunctious affair, a far cry from the polite conversation at the Brookes' breakfast table.

"Use your napkin, Robbie," Lindsay instructed as the boy lowered his glass to reveal a milk mustache.

Miss Manners, Ryder thought, oddly pleased that aspect of Lindsay's personality hadn't changed. Her automatic corrections and know-it-all attitude had led some kids to believe she was something of a snob, but he'd always gotten a kick out of how smart she was.

Which made him wonder…

"So, what kind of work do you do, Lindsay?"

"I work for a PR firm in Phoenix."

"Really?"

He couldn't keep the surprise from his voice, and judging by the way her chin rose, Lindsay heard it. "Yes, really. I've been there for five years now."

Ryder had always known Lindsay would succeed at whatever she chose to do even after he heard she'd gotten pregnant. But he'd always figured the shy, studious girl he'd known would grow up to be a librarian or a computer whiz or an accountant, where she'd be somewhat behind the scenes, using her brain to problem-solve.

Not that PR work didn't require serious problem-solving skills. He'd seen on a professional level how his in-laws' used their PR team to divert and deflect any negative publicity away from the firm and also on a personal level as Brittany put so much spin on their divorce that the truth had become an indecipherable blur.

Not that he cared. At least, not all that much. He'd rather be the jerk who walked out on his marriage than the schmuck whose wife had been lying to him for years.

"My mom's been on TV and everything."

Robbie offered up that information, pulling Ryder from the past and bringing his focus back to what really surprised him about Lindsay's career choice. "On TV and everything," he echoed. She certainly had looked television-ready the day before, and that was while picking up pizza at a fast-food joint.

The old Lindsay would have blushed at his teasing, but the new Lindsay met his grin with a wry smile of her own. "Local news and a cable television talk show," she said, dismissing it as no big deal, though her son was obviously impressed.

So was Ryder, since as far as he knew, Lindsay's only less than stellar grade in high school came after she bailed in the middle of an oral history presentation. She'd stuttered, words tripping one over the other, until she simply froze, horrified, her face pale as her mouth opened and closed with no words coming out, no air going in, drowning in humiliation—

Another memory stabbed at him. Lindsay standing beside his locker, waiting for him on the Monday morning following that fateful weekend. Standing beside his locker and looking even more horrified, more humiliated, more *hurt*.

Suddenly, despite the delicious food still on his plate, Ryder couldn't swallow another bite.

He'd felt bad about it, but hell, maybe he was the one who should have gone into the spit-and-polish world of PR. Hadn't he glossed over what he'd done, justifying his actions with the best of them, until he'd convinced himself his own BS was the God's honest truth?

He was protecting her by keeping what happened a secret…

It would only make matters worse if the truth came out…

Lindsay might not understand, but he was doing what was best for everyone…

He'd believed every line he told himself, because at the time, he hadn't known what it felt like to suffer that kind of betrayal, that kind of manipulation.

He knew now.

Thanks to Brittany, to the secret she'd revealed during their final fight—*"I did it for us!"*—he knew the shock and pain of having the world pulled out from beneath his feet.

Maybe it was ten years too late, and maybe Lindsay no longer gave a damn, but he owed her an apology. And if fixing up the house meant Lindsay and her folks didn't have to worry about Ellie stumbling on the uneven front steps or losing her balance when leaning too hard on rickety railing—two of the problems he'd noticed on the way inside—well, that was the least he could do.

But there was something Lindsay needed to know, something her grandmother evidently hadn't told her…

"Can—may I be excused?" Robbie asked. At his mother's nod, he added, "And go play video games on your tablet?"

"Sure." Lindsay exhaled the word on a sigh, her shoulders relaxing a bit for the first time since Ryder had stepped foot inside the kitchen.

"Really?" The boy popped up from his chair as though he thought she might change her mind any second. "Cool!"

"Clear off your dishes first, and thank your Grandma Ellie for breakfast."

"Thanks, Gran," the boy parroted before he grabbed his plate and glass, carried them to the sink and ducked out of the kitchen, his feet pounding the stairs as he raced upstairs.

"Kid sure likes his video games, huh?" Ryder asked, remembering how the boy had cried out in excitement before nearly running him down in his haste to get to the games at the pizza parlor.

Lindsay's gaze cut from the kitchen doorway her son had disappeared through to lock on to his. "The *kid's* name is Robbie."

"Right. Sure. Robbie. He seems like a great kid," he said, cringing a little even as he said the word, half expecting Lindsay to go all mama bear again even though he didn't have a clue why she'd gotten so defensive in the first place.

"He is. He's smart and sweet and funny and—" Her words broke off as she turned her focus back to her plate and the food she'd barely touched.

Ellie made a sympathetic sound as she explained, "Robbie's a bit on the shy side, and Lindsay worries people won't see him for the amazing boy he is."

"I'm not worried," Lindsay argued.

"Of course you are, dear. You're a mother. It's your job to worry. But I have the feeling this trip is going to do him a world of good. You'll see." Before Lindsay's puzzled frown had time to set in, Ellie waved a hand at the spread still in front of them. "So, are either of you up for seconds?"

"No, thank you, Mrs. Brookes. But that's gotta be the best meal I've had in ages."

"Oh, you're welcome. And please call me Ellie."

He rose as Lindsay's grandmother did and reached for his own plate. "Let me give you a hand with the rest of these."

"Aren't you a sweetheart!"

If he thought he'd gain any points with his offer, he'd have been bound for disappointment as Lindsay rolled her eyes at Ellie's effusive comment.

Waving aside his attempt to help her clean up, Ellie said, "I can handle things in here if you two would like to get started."

"The two of us…" Lindsay echoed.

"You're the one always going on about the work that needs to be done around here. Who better to show Ryder around?"

"Right." Lindsay sighed. "Because this was all my big idea."

With Ellie once again waving them out of the kitchen, Lindsay led the way back into the living room. Her messy ponytail bobbed in time with her steps, and Ryder couldn't keep his gaze drifting from her slender shoulders, to her narrow waist and curving hips. She turned quickly, but not so quickly, he hoped, that she caught where his eye had wandered.

"Look, just because my grandmother invited you over, that doesn't mean we're hiring you."

"Fair enough. After all, you still have those references to verify."

"That's right." Her shoulders straightened as she met his gaze. "And I want to consider other bids, as well. I've already done some checking around. I saw an advertisement for Parker Remodeling—"

"Travis Parker." Ryder scowled at the man's name. "You don't want to hire him."

"Why not? You're not afraid of a little competition, are you?"

"Parker isn't competition. What he is is a first-class womanizer with a reputation for not taking no for an answer."

Lindsay blinked in surprise, taken aback by his warning tone. "Well, I can take care of myself. I have been for a long time now."

Ryder knew that was probably truer than he could imagine. But that didn't mean he liked the idea of her having to fend off a guy like Travis Parker. Not that he was entirely sure why the thought of the notorious player hitting on Lindsay bothered him as much as it did.

He was looking out for her. Protecting Lindsay— Hell, protecting her in a way he hadn't protected her from himself ten years ago. He owed her that much, though judging by the way she lifted her chin a stubborn notch, she wasn't going to make it easy on him.

"Still, I'm sure there's another handyman in town."

Handyman. Right. "Look, Lindsay, about that…I'm not exactly a handyman. I was hired by a contracting company to work on remodeling projects—like what you probably have in mind for updating this place."

Her brow furrowed at the warning in his voice. "Okay."

"The thing is—the company I work for—it's Pirelli Construction. Drew Pirelli's company. I wanted you to know in case you thought it made things, you know, too complicated."

"Too complicated."

Lindsay blinked as Ryder's words sank in, and that hysterical laughter rose in her throat again. Complicated? What could possibly be complicated about hiring the father of her child, who worked for the cousin of the man everyone *thought* was the father of her child?

Not to mention fixing up the house so her grandmother would be even more convinced she should stay in the old Victorian when the entire goal had been to get the place ready to sell?

Oh, no. No complications there at all.

"It's a solid company, Lindsay, and I do good work," Ryder vowed. "You won't be sorry."

But she already was, wasn't she? Seeing Robbie and Ryder together for the first time had hit her harder than she'd imagined. From the moment her son was born, it had just been the two of them. Her parents and grandparents had supported her, and Lindsay didn't know what she would have done without them. But she had been the only parent Robbie had known. She'd never faced the thought of sharing him. Of letting him go, even the smallest amount, because he'd always been hers alone.

The fear and uncertainty churning inside her were almost enough to make Lindsay want to grab Robbie and race back to Phoenix. And then Ryder stepped closer, and something…more was added to the mix of emotions. Something that held her in place despite that urge to run.

His gaze searched her face, and there was no sign of the teasing grin he'd flashed her way earlier. If anything, his expression was more serious than she'd ever seen, guilt and regret pulling at his handsome features. "I know with everything that happened between us, I don't really have the right to ask. But all I'm looking for is a chance to prove I'm not the same guy I was in high school."

Chapter Four

A few days later, Ryder's words were still playing through Lindsay's mind. That was what she wanted, too, wasn't it? For Ryder to prove himself. Not to her, because this couldn't be about her and it certainly couldn't be about that *something* she'd felt when he stood so close to her in grandmother's living room. No, this had to be about Ryder proving he could be someone Robbie could trust, someone he could count on.

Even if their relationship would be a long-distance one, even if—heaven help her—that relationship would be limited to a few weeks over summer vacation, spring break, and joint custody for every other holiday, Lindsay couldn't deny that Robbie needed a father in his life.

And Ryder deserved a chance to show her that he could be that father.

Which was why she was putting the finishing touches on her makeup with a hand that trembled ever so slightly.

"Stop it!" she hissed at her own reflection. "This isn't a date."

Despite the warning, Lindsay's pulse jumped at every sound coming from downstairs, though so far she heard nothing more than her gran making breakfast. She'd go down to help but only after getting dressed and making sure every strand of hair was perfectly in place. Ryder Kincaid was not catching her with her beagle slippers on again.

As promised, he'd left her with a list of references as well as his initial quote once Lindsay showed him the work that needed to be done. She cringed when she thought of all the additional problems Ryder had found. She'd called around checking those references, relieved to have found names on the list she didn't recognize. Word would get out soon enough that she had hired Pirelli Construction, but Lindsay wasn't looking forward to explaining.

Another point for life in Phoenix, where she didn't have to explain. Where people accepted that she was a single mom and rarely bothered to ask questions that couldn't be waved away with nothing more than a simple "it was a long time ago" response.

Even Robbie had stopped asking questions about who his father was...

Underneath Lindsay's relief, though, was a niggling concern. Shouldn't her son be more curious? Years ago, she had explained that his father was an old friend from Clearville who wasn't a part of their lives. But Robbie had always been an inquisitive kid, the type to keep asking "why?" long after Lindsay had run out of answers.

At an age when Lindsay had braced herself for more questions, Robbie remained silent. Of course, he had plenty of classmates with divorced parents or who lived in single-parent homes. Maybe Robbie had simply accepted that it was just the two of them.

But as Lindsay skipped down the stairs, a low masculine murmur reminded her that it wasn't just the two of them. At least not right now. How had she missed Ryder's arrival? Easily enough, she figured, deciding her grand-mother had probably told him to let himself in. No need to knock and who bothered to lock their doors in little ol' Clearville?

Chalk it up to living in Phoenix too long, but she was adding installing a dead bolt to Ryder's list of things to do.

"And see here?" Ellie was asking. "My Robert installed these lovely wall sconces. Sometimes you have to jiggle them a bit before they work…"

Oh, shoot. She'd wanted the chance to warn Ryder that the "shoddy craftsmanship" another contractor had kept pointing out to her over and over had been done by her grandfather. It would break her grandmother's heart to hear the work her grandfather had taken such pride in de-scribed that way.

Ryder and Ellie were standing beneath the somewhat gaudy gilded and glass lamps—her gran in a pair of sea-foam-green capris and a beige T-shirt with floral appli-qués across the front, Ryder towering over her in jeans and a navy T-shirt. Lindsay swallowed hard, her plan to interrupt their conversation stalling as the words—and her very breath—lodged in her throat at the sight of him.

He'd braced his hands above the tool belt hanging low on his lean hips, the muscles in his arms flexed beneath tanned skin. The masculine stance emphasized the breadth of his shoulders, flat stomach and long legs. His posture spoke of confidence—maybe even a bit of cockiness—and Lindsay waited, dreading the moment when he would say—

"I can see by all the work your husband did around here that he must have loved this place very much."

Lindsay sucked in a soft breath even as unexpected tears stung her eyes. She would have instructed Ryder not to say anything about the workmanship, but the words he'd chosen were far better than a telling silence. He'd been completely honest and yet, at the same time, had managed not to criticize her grandfather.

Lindsay didn't know if he'd heard the sound she'd made, but he glanced over his shoulder. He shot her a quick, conspiratorial wink as if the two of them were in this together. Both of them out to preserve the wonderful old Victorian as well as her grandfather's memory. The press of tears gathered behind her eyes along with a pressure in her chest, and Lindsay sucked in a deep breath before all that emotion could build up into a soft sob.

Together. Working as a team. She...and Ryder.

It was almost overwhelming, and Lindsay steeled herself against the weakness. A split-second shared moment wasn't enough to close a ten-year gap or give her insight into the man Ryder was now. And it certainly wasn't enough of a foundation to build a father-son relationship on.

You're not a silly teenager anymore. It's going to take more than a sexy wink and a teasing smile.

She was a mother now, not some starry-eyed girl. She was a responsible adult. She was...a healthy, young woman who hadn't been on the receiving end of a sexy wink in far, far too long. Or at least that was what her body seemed to say as Ryder's appreciative gaze swept over her. Her stomach trembled ever so slightly and it was all she could do not to give away the telling reaction by crossing her arms at her waist. As if she could keep the suddenly wild butterflies there from busting out and filling the room with their colorful, fluttering wings.

"Oh, yes," Ellie was saying. "And it was so good for him to have something to keep him busy after he retired. I know when you're young, retirement sounds like this wonderful, long vacation, but it's not always easy to realize the work you've taken such pride in for so many years is going on without you and that, well, you simply aren't needed anymore."

The tremor in her grandmother's voice snapped Lindsay's focus back in place like a quick head slap. She had a reason for coming to Clearville, and it wasn't to start mooning over Ryder Kincaid. Ellie *was* needed, and her grandmother would realize how much life still had to offer once she'd moved to Phoenix with her family.

"Morning, Gran," she said brightly as she stepped into the living room.

"Oh, Lindsay. There you are, dear. I was telling Ryder you would have been down sooner if you didn't dress like you expect to be on television every day."

Heat flooded her face as she met her gran's smile. Ryder's grin grew even bigger as he whispered in a not so subtle aside, "All that fame went to her head, huh?"

Ellie sighed. "She may well be too good for us both."

"Okay, stop. Both of you," Lindsay argued even though she couldn't help giving a little chuckle.

Too good for Ryder Kincaid. That was actually worthy of a gut-busting belly laugh, but somehow Lindsay lost the humor she'd found in the moment.

"I dress like a professional because I am a professional. Nothing more to it than that." Last thing Lindsay needed was for Ryder to know how she'd agonized over her wardrobe—far more stressed than when she *had* dressed to be on television—before finally settling on a pair of ivory slacks and a sleeveless buttery-yellow blouse with rows of ruffles from the high neckline down to the fitted waistline. She'd added a pair of strappy beige sandals rather than her usual heels and kept her makeup and jewelry to a minimum. After all, she didn't want Ryder to think she was dressing up because of him.

Even if she was.

"You're on vacation," her grandmother emphasized. "You should dress like you're on vacation. You need to relax a little, have some fun. Ryder, maybe while Lindsay is in town, you could take her out a night or two. She really hasn't—"

"Gran!" The last thing she needed was her grandmother's matchmaking! "Ryder is here because we've hired him to do a job. Taking me out to dinner is not part of his scope of work."

"No, that would definitely be an added benefit," Ryder murmured much to her grandmother's delight.

"Don't you have breakfast to make for a growing boy who's going to wake up starving any minute now?" Lindsay asked, ignoring everything she'd told Ellie over the past few days about Robbie's ability to fend for himself.

"Oh, yes. Ryder, you're welcome to join us again."

"Thanks, Ellie, but I think I'd better get started on the work you're paying me to do."

"All right, then, but remember the offer still stands."

Her grandmother gave a small wave as she walked back toward the kitchen, and Lindsay's relief that she and Ryder no longer had a matchmaking audience faded as she realized the two of them were now alone.

Alone for the first time since *that night* over ten years ago.

Oh, sure, they'd spoken briefly the other day, but this time Lindsay wasn't ushering Ryder out the door. He was here to stay. For the next several weeks based on the estimate she'd signed. And she would have to deal with him invading her space, with seeing him every day...

"I wouldn't worry too much about what your grandmother said. You look amazing."

Lindsay swallowed as Ryder's green gaze swept from the top of her head and the hair she'd pulled up in a twist and down to her feet. Every inch in between tingled in awareness, and his familiar smile set those butterflies to fluttering again.

"Even if I do miss the beagle slippers and glasses."

Flames licked her cheeks at his teasing, but there was something in his voice, something that made Lindsay think—Ryder couldn't possibly have found her *more* attractive in her ridiculous beagle slippers, ponytail and pajamas, could he? Couldn't be hinting that he liked the old version of her—the shy, awkward girl she'd been—better than the new, improved woman she'd fought so hard to become?

She forced the question out of her mind. Ryder's preference didn't matter. She hadn't changed for him. She'd made the transformation for herself and for Robbie. She might have been a young, single mother, but she'd been determined to hold her head high and to let her son know she wasn't ashamed of him.

Ignoring the beagle slippers comment altogether, she asked, "What's on the agenda for today?"

"I thought I'd start on the front porch. The stairs—the stringers and the steps—all need to be remade along with the railing. We're supposed to have some good weather the next few days, so that's a plus for working outdoors."

Clearville weather—while far cooler than the summers she'd gotten used to in Phoenix—could be mercurial. In the desert, you could count on long, hot, rain-free days throughout May and June with the monsoon storms holding off until July or August. But the Northern California weather was less predictable with occasional rain and fog rolling in off the nearby ocean.

"I'll replace the porch fascia, and I want to strip the paint off the floorboards, too."

Lindsay tried not to grimace at the amount of work—and that was only the outside. "What color were you thinking of repainting?" Her grandfather had gone with a mottled grayish green that she figured must have been on sale but, unfortunately, clashed with the house's pale blue gingerbread trim.

"I figured I'd stain it. Keep it natural, you know. Why cover up perfection?"

And there it was again. That low murmur and the look in his eyes that set off a trembling in her belly and sudden weakness in her knees. Lindsay swallowed even as she tried desperately to pull her gaze from his. That might have worked if she hadn't found even more tempting features to focus on—the high curve of his cheekbones, the hint of stubble along his jaw, the sculpted perfection of his lips, so close to hers. Lips that looked so sexy and seductive—

"Of course, I'll have to tear out any warped or rotted pieces."

Warped and— Right. The porch. All that talk about keeping things natural. Not covering up perfection. And she'd actually thought he'd been talking about her?

Lindsay Anne Brookes, how big a fool are you?

There didn't seem to be an answer to that question, so she chose to respond to Ryder instead. "I like the idea of keeping the natural wood on the porch. What about the railing and—fascia, wasn't it?"

He nodded. "I'll try to match that with the trim on the house or we could add another color if your grandmother would like that."

"Matching the trim would be best." Although the painted ladies, as the Victorian houses were called, often had a variety of colors along the trim, eaves and fascia, Lindsay didn't want to go overboard. She had to keep the new buyer in mind. "I do want to thank you," she said to Ryder, "for being so…sensitive about my gran's feelings and the work my grandfather did."

"Me? Sensitive? Wow. Can you write that down so I

can show my mother? I don't think she'll believe it without proof."

"It was a bit of a shock to me, too."

Because there'd been a time when the way Ryder treated her had been anything but sensitive.

The unspoken reminder of the past swirled around them, obscuring the teasing moment. Ryder's expression sobered. "Lindsay—"

Her stomach clenched. She didn't know what he was going to say, but she suddenly didn't want to hear it. Not now. Not when she still had to face seeing him on a daily basis for weeks to come. "Anyway, I appreciate it. My grandfather did love this place and put a lot of hard work into it. Even if his skill didn't match his determination."

"Well, there's no reason for me to go around bad-mouthing the work he did, but you do know that I'm going to have to start over with most of it, right? The porch is only the beginning, but once I'm done, your gran won't have to worry about uneven steps or a loose railing anymore."

"I appreciate that, but it really isn't my grandmother you'll be fixing the place up for. Once the repairs are complete, we're going to put the house up on the market. My parents and I think it's time for Ellie to move to Phoenix to be with us."

"Really? What does Ellie think about that?"

Lindsay smiled with a confidence she was far from feeling. "You work on the house, and I'll work on my grandmother. It'll take some convincing, but in the end, she'll see that moving to Phoenix is the best thing for her."

Chapter Five

Most days, Ryder loved working with his hands. Crafting something brand-new or better yet, improving what already existed. He had plenty of opportunities remodeling the old Victorians. Craftsmanship that had stood the test of time and Mother Nature—including the occasional earthquake—couldn't be found in modern, cookie-cutter track homes. Or even in the high-rises he'd designed back in San Francisco.

Yeah, most days he loved building. But other days— he eyed the wobbly railing on Ellie Brookes's front porch and gave the wood a solid kick. The shock traveled all the way up his spine along with the satisfying crack of splintering wood.

Other days, mass destruction fit his mood.

Not that he had any reason to feel so…angry. Another blow against the banister with his work boot and another split accompanied by the groan from the rusty old nails. Should have used screws, he thought. But if Lindsay's grandfather had built a sturdier railing, he wouldn't have been able to kick the thing down. Might not have needed to kick the damn thing down. Which would have been good for the Brookes, but not so good for him. Because he really felt the need to kick something.

You're acting like an ass.

He knew it. But he also knew it was better to act like an ass when no one was watching than to let his feelings boil over as they almost had last night.

Ryder swore beneath his breath and reared back again just thinking of how close he'd come to ruining what had been an exciting and wonderful moment for his brother and sister-in-law.

He'd gone over to their place for dinner as he had so many nights since his return. He liked his rental for hitting the hay after a long day at work. The house had come furnished with an oversize recliner and flat-screen TV, so the living room suited him just fine for catching a ball game on the weekend. But the kitchen—with its large, eat-in nook and table that easily seated six—yeah, there was something about eating every meal alone there that Ryder couldn't stomach.

So he'd been over at his brother's a lot. And not once had Bryce or Nina complained. *"You're family. We're glad you're here."*

But he'd be willing to bet they wouldn't have been nearly so glad if they'd known how he felt when they made their big announcement last night...

Nina had been late coming home from work—she'd had to make a stop, Bryce had explained, his voice a little funny now that Ryder was looking back. But at the time, he hadn't thought anything of it. Instead he'd given his brother a hand with grilling the burgers outside and keeping an eye on Tyler and Brayden, his two rambunctious nephews, and their equally rambunctious dog—a black-and-white border collie mix with energy to spare.

And it was a good thing he'd been there, because Bryce had been more than a little distracted. Checking his watch every few minutes and glancing back at the house almost as often. And then Nina had come home.

Ryder heard the slap of the screen door and had glanced over after tossing the football to his youngest nephew. His automatic greeting died on his lips when he caught sight of his sister-in-law's face. She'd stood on the back stoop, her hand pressed against her chest, her cheeks flushed and tears shimmering in her eyes. Even without knowing what was going on, Ryder froze.

He'd watched as Bryce abandoned the grill, leaving the burgers sizzling and smoking away to walk slowly toward his wife. He was still a few steps away when a trembling smile transformed Nina's expression and she gave a quick, happy nod.

That was all it took for Bryce to let out a war whoop that would have done his sons proud before he bounded up the back steps and swept his wife into his arms. Nina had started laughing and crying, the boys and the dog had come running, attracted by the noise and excitement, and by then Ryder had had a feeling of what was coming.

"We're having a baby!" his brother had announced, his jubilant voice filling the entire backyard.

The boys had both cheered and groaned, exciting by the prospect but already grossed out by the idea of poopy diapers. And Ryder had joined the group, slapping his brother on the back in a male version of a hug and kissing his sister-in-law's cheek. He'd smiled and said all the right things, but then he'd made his excuses and left with the burgers still popping on the grill.

"Tonight's about your family. You should all share this moment," he'd told Bryce.

Naturally his brother had insisted that Ryder was family, too. But it wasn't *his* family. Not his sons, not his dog, not his pregnant wife…

And he'd known he wouldn't be able to keep his smile in place for long. That Bryce or Nina would pick up on the envy and bitterness and anger he still couldn't shake. That the ugliness of his emotions would cast a shadow over the couple's sheer happiness, and Ryder insisted that he should go. He'd congratulated them a final time and offered his hope that, after two boys, they might have girl.

A boy or a girl…

There'd been a time when Ryder would have been happy with either.

"Why don't you use your truck?"

The inquisitive remark caught Ryder off guard and mid-kick. He nearly missed the railing and might have taken a header right off the porch if he hadn't grabbed hold of the support post.

Catching his balance and his breath, Ryder glanced over his shoulder. Lindsay's son had slipped out the front door and stood behind him, watching with a serious, unblinking gaze behind his wire-rimmed glasses.

"My truck?" he echoed, not sure what the kid wanted to use the vehicle for.

"You know, tie a rope from the railing to the thingie on your bumper." The boy lifted a skinny shoulder beneath a red T-shirt that hung on his narrow frame. "Be faster."

"Easier, too, huh?" he asked, though easy hadn't exactly been what he was going for. He'd wanted the hard work to burn off the emotions that had built up inside him until he could beat them back into the past where they belonged.

"Uh-huh." Despite the agreement, Robbie crossed the porch to stand beside Ryder, where he, too, kicked at the railing with a scuffed-up sneaker. He gave it a good try, his too-long bangs and glasses flopping with the effort, though the railing barely moved.

It was enough to make Ryder smile. "Think we should try the easy way?"

"Yeah, or me and my mom are gonna be here a long time."

"You don't like it here?"

Another one-shoulder shrug. "It's kinda boring."

"No kids to play with?" he asked, figuring he knew the answer when the boy dogged his heels as he strode toward his truck and grabbed a chain from the lockbox in the back. Something he should have done in the first place. He'd backed the truck up to the front porch to limit the trek he'd need to make to dump the old, warped boards into the bed for hauling them off, so the vehicle was already close enough to do the job.

"Dunno."

Ryder figured that meant the boy hadn't actually checked out the neighborhood. When he'd been a kid, a lot of the Victorians were occupied by people he and his friends had joked were old enough to be the original owners. But many of the neighborhoods had been revitalized— the houses updated on the inside while maintaining their century-plus charm on the outside—and the many rooms were filled with young families.

Families like Bryce and Nina's...

Steeling himself against the kick in the gut that did far more damage than he'd managed to inflict on the front porch, Ryder focused on Lindsay's boy. "You know, my brother has two sons right around your age."

Instead of the interest he'd expected, the information earned Ryder another shrug. The kid was clearly a tough nut to crack—like his mother. Lindsay's studied seriousness had always brought out the devil in him, challenging

Ryder to break through the reserved shell she showed the rest of the world and find the real girl underneath.

Now it was her aloof, professional veneer that dared him to push past those boundaries. But they weren't kids anymore, and Lindsay was a single mother. Still, that didn't mean she couldn't let loose and have fun some of the time. Even her grandmother thought so, as Ryder hadn't missed Ellie's hint that he take Lindsay out for a night on the town. Or at least Clearville's version of a night out, which was usually nothing more than dinner and a beer at the Bar and Grille.

Maybe he should ask her out—as friends and for old times' sake. Ryder certainly wasn't looking for anything more than that. Not after the job Brittany's designer heels had done on his heart.

Turning his attention back to Robbie, he said, "Pretty smart of you to think of using the truck." He handed the balance of the chain to the wide-eyed boy to hold while he threaded the links between the railing spindles. Ryder had already cut away the braces from the support columns before he'd gone all Bruce Lee on the railing. No reason to pull the whole porch away from the front of the house.

"Your mom was always the smartest person I knew in school."

"Yeah, she's pretty smart, but sometimes she still treats me like a kid."

"Go figure."

Missing the wry undertones, Robbie nodded. "Yeah." He sighed.

Linking the one end of the chain, Ryder motioned for Robbie to string the rest along the ground while he connected the other end to the hitch on the bumper.

"Okay, I'm gonna need your help now." Pointing toward the driveway, well out of range of the truck and the chain, he said, "I need you to stand over there and tell me when the chain pulls tight, okay?"

Robbie nodded with all seriousness before racing to take his spot. "I'm ready!"

It was a trick Ryder had learned from watching Bryce and his sons—finding a way to include the boys in his "man projects" as Nina liked to call them while still keeping them out of harm's way. Yeah, his older brother was a great father and a great husband with a strong, loving marriage to show for it.

While Ryder—all he had to show for the past ten years of his life was a failed college football career, an ex-wife and a bitter divorce. As for kids… The engine roared to life as he stepped on the gas with more force than necessary. Maybe Brittany was right. Maybe it was all for the best.

Lindsay touched the screen on her tablet, flipping to another page of houses for sale. She wanted to get a good idea what Victorians like her grandmother's were going for. The asking prices in some cases were staggering, but from what she could see, those houses were "Tour of Homes"–ready and didn't show any of the wear and tear the old place displayed.

Her eyebrows rose at a picture of a drawing room so ornately furnished it looked more like a museum. She couldn't imagine anyone actually living in a house decorated with such precision. She certainly couldn't picture her grandmother there.

She glanced around the sunroom at the back of the house, every free space filled with her grandmother's knickknacks and overflowing with plants. White wicker furniture filled the space. Along with the two-person lounge where Lindsay sat, matching rocking chairs flanked a coffee table along with half a dozen or so mismatched end tables that served as plant stands. Garden statuary was tucked in between the blooming African violets, trailing ivy and philodendron—a small bunny here, a fat cherub there, a smiling frog nearly hidden in the corner.

The exterior wall was windows from the wainscot up, but Ellie still found places to hang small items—a round daisy-faced thermometer, a floral stained glass suncatcher and a few tins painted with flowers, watering cans and picket fences with cutesy sayings like How Does Your Garden Grow?

The room was so Ellie—and so not HGTV. Lindsay had watched enough shows to know what the staging and real estate experts would say about the house.

Declutter, depersonalize.

She could imagine the battle that would ensue when she tried to convince Ellie. And even she had to admit that part of the home's charm, part of its character, were her gran's personal touches.

Ignoring the slight ache in her chest, Lindsay focused on the website. It had to be done. Once Ellie moved to Phoenix and saw all the options available in a city known for winter visitors and senior living, she'd be relieved not to have the huge responsibility of a large and aging house.

Now all Lindsay had to do was cross her fingers that the repairs went as quickly and smoothly as possible.

Right, her subconscious taunted. *Because you can't hide out in the sunroom forever.*

As much as she would have liked to deny the needling voice, it was no coincidence that she'd retreated to a room at the back of the house. As far away from the front porch, where Ryder worked, as she could get without leaving altogether.

Keeping her distance definitely seemed…safer. Especially after her brief foray into the front parlor earlier that morning. She'd gone into the room to retrieve the tablet Robbie had left there, but instead of picking up the small electronic device sitting on the coffee table, she'd let her steps carry her straight toward the window.

She'd stood, spellbound, watching as Ryder did nothing more than measure the porch. He'd laid out the tape one end to the other and pulled a pencil out from behind his ear to make a note on a pad of paper he then stuffed into his back pocket. And that was where Lindsay's gaze had stayed, glued to his jeans as he'd squatted down to examine the railing at eye level, the worn denim pulling tight over his muscular backside and thighs.

She didn't know how long she would have stared out at him, a slow flush stealing over her—both at the sight of the man Ryder had grown into and in embarrassment over being such a…a voyeur—if he hadn't pushed to his feet and turned in her direction. The idea of getting caught gawking at him as if they were still teenagers—as if *she* were still a gawky teenager—had her spinning away from the window and hoping her grandmother's white lace curtains had shielded her from his view.

Even now, an hour or so later, safely tucked away from temptation, Lindsay's face still felt hot. How could he do this to her after ten years? After the way he'd treated her, how could she still…want him?

Old insecurities threatened to wash over her like the waves on the beach, pulling her in deeper and deeper until she no longer had the will to fight, but she'd come too far to allow that to happen. So maybe she did still find Ryder…irresistible.

Attractive, she mentally corrected. He was an attractive man, but she *would* resist. And if sheer avoidance was her main tactic for that resistance, well, whatever worked, right? Out of sight, out of mind and all that.

At least she'd managed the first half.

She'd determinedly refocused her efforts on the real estate website when the roar of an engine startled her. *What on earth?* The thought barely registered before a wrenching, cracking sound followed, loud enough to make her fear the whole house was about to fall down. And then a cry that shot terror straight through her heart.

"Robbie!"

She tossed the tablet aside and scrambled off the love seat cushion. Her heart pounded as if she'd raced a mile before she even made it out of the sunroom. She threw open the front door and stared in shock at the destruction. One side of the railing was ripped away from the porch with only a few sharp shards of spindles remaining. The rest had been dragged several feet across the lawn in a twisted tangle of wood and chain and bent over right in the middle was her son.

"Are you okay? What happened? Are you hurt?" Lindsay raced down the porch steps toward her son, stumbling and stepping over debris in her haste. She gasped as she lost her balance, heart stopping as she had a split-second awareness of the broken spikes of wood on the ground, sticking up with daggerlike sharpness.

"Whoa! Hold on!" Ryder reached out, a solid, muscular arm grasping her waist as he hauled her back against his chest. A warm gust of breath teased the side of her neck as he asked, "You okay?"

Her own near miss was nothing compared to her worry for her son. "Robbie! Is he—"

"He's fine," Ryder reassured her, and Lindsay could see that her son had already pushed to his feel and was staring wide-eyed at her. Her gaze raked over him, head to toe, and other than what appeared to be some kind of grease stain on the front of his shirt and across one skinny forearm, he was perfectly fine.

Exhaling a shaky sigh, she slumped back against Ryder's chest. Only then, with the heat of his body pressed against hers, did she realize he hadn't let her go yet. If anything his grip had shifted ever so slightly from catching her to…holding her. His arm rested below her breasts, and his hand had curved around her rib cage. His long legs were braced on either side of hers, and she could feel the solid press of denim through the lightweight material of her beige linen slacks.

"Are you okay?"

The shiver that raced down her spine at his low murmur, more than the words themselves, shook Lindsay out of her stupor. Jerking out of his grasp, cursing the weakness in her still-trembling legs, she whirled to face him. "Forget about me! What were you doing tearing away the side of the house with my son right in the middle of everything!"

"Mom!"

Ignoring Robbie's embarrassed protest, she said, "He could have been seriously injured, Ryder! What were you thinking?"

Ryder reached for her shoulders, but she stepped back, evading his touch. His eyebrows pulled low, but his voice was placating as he said, "He's fine, Lindsay, and he was never in any danger. You don't need to worry."

"Don't tell me not to worry. I'm his mother. He's—"

My son.

Her voice cut out suddenly, her throat closing around the words that were the truth…but not the whole truth.

"I know that, and do you really think I would ever let anything happen to him?" Ryder asked softly, as if he would take extra precautions with Robbie, caring for the boy because he cared for her.

But that was ridiculous. After all this time, she and Ryder were practically strangers. They'd never really been much more than strangers, her crush in high school and one ill-fated night of passion not enough to form the basis for any kind of relationship.

"I was standing over there the whole time, Mom! So I

could tell Mr. Ryder when the chain pulled tight." Even Robbie seemed to realize the precautions Ryder had taken to keep him away from danger. "It was my idea to use the truck, and it was awesome!"

His voice rose at the end, explaining the cry she'd heard earlier. Exuberance, not injury, and Lindsay stared in surprise at the animation lighting his face. She hadn't seen him this excited away from a video game in—she didn't know how long. All because Ryder had included him. Of course, it probably didn't hurt that the job had involved some major demolition. What nine-year-old boy wouldn't be impressed?

That wasn't enough to still the flutters of panic beating around her heart, but Lindsay sucked in a deep breath. This was a good thing. Part of coming back to Clearville had been for this very reason—for Robbie to get to know his father. But like that moment when she saw the boy standing in a dangerous pile of debris, surrounded by splintering wood and rusty nails, she couldn't help feeling as though she needed to pull him away from the potential dangers.

"I don't want him to get hurt," she whispered, wrapping her arms around her waist.

"Hey, I get it," Ryder said, and Lindsay blinked, confused for a second, until she realized she'd spoken the words out loud.

But instead of reassuring her, Ryder's words seemed all too carefree. "Do you? What do you know about raising a child?"

A muscle jumped in his jaw as he shook his head. "Not a damn thing. But I do know what it's like being a boy and that you can't protect him forever. At some point he's going to have to stop living inside video games or hiding from the world by burying his head in a book."

Heat licked along her cheekbones at his words and at the look in his eyes, a look that called up every memory

Lindsay had of the painfully shy high school days where, yes, she'd tried as hard as possible to lose herself in the pages of rich and exciting fiction rather than face the reality of everyday life.

"Plus, I have two nephews," Ryder was saying. "So while I don't know about raising a child, I at least know a thing or two about keeping them involved and out of harm's way."

"Can we do the other side now?" Robbie called out, clearly bored with waiting around while the adults talked. He kicked at a piece of wood, and Lindsay ground her back teeth together to keep from calling out to him to be careful. To stay back. To warn him about tetanus and lockjaw and a whole list of other concerns no nine-year-old boy cared about.

Still, she said, "I don't know if it's a good idea for you to be out here while Mr. Ryder's working."

His shoulders dropped as he turned to face her. "Oh, come on, Mom! You're always trying to get me to do guy stuff with Grandpa back home. Why can't I help Mr. Ryder with Grandma Ellie's house?"

Ryder raised an eyebrow. Great, nothing like her son outing the fact that Lindsay was trying to provide a male influence in her son's life. Or that her own father was the best she could do.

I don't know a damn thing about raising a child.

Was it guilt that had her hearing the slice of anger or... hurt undercutting those words? Ryder didn't know—couldn't know—that Lindsay's own silence had taken the chance of raising a child—their child—away from him. And yet she didn't think she'd simply imagined the ripples beneath Ryder's flat, emotionless tone.

And suddenly Lindsay sensed how important this moment was. Not just for Robbie, to give him time with the man who was his father, but also for Ryder. To show him...

"I trust you," Lindsay whispered, the words barely able to escape on a breath beyond the lump in her throat.

Ryder glanced at her with a quizzical frown, and she forced herself to repeat the words. Louder and with enough certainty to convince the both of them they were true. "I trust you. With Robbie. If you don't mind him hanging out while you work…"

"No, I don't mind," he responded, sounding a little surprised by the realization. "And I meant what I said. I'll watch for him, Lindsay."

"Yes, well, I'll be watching, too," she murmured. "Just to make sure."

"Ah, of course." But if the idea of her "supervising" bothered Ryder, his one-sided grin and the light in his eyes certainly didn't let it show. "Gotta warn you, remodeling an old house like this isn't as glamorous as they make it look on television, and sure can't be done in a day or over a weekend."

"I'm well aware of the amount of work the place needs."

"Right. After all, you got all those quotes from other contractors."

Lindsay willed herself not to smile, not to give in to the dare behind Ryder's teasing grin. "Like you said, I always do my homework."

"Checked all the references, too, didn't you?"

"That's right. Had a fascinating conversation with a Mrs. Webber." With the way the woman had gushed over Ryder, Lindsay almost would have suspected the two of them had a thing going on—if Widow Webber hadn't sounded as though she was eighty-five if she was a day.

"Yep. Helped her out with a broken pipe." Ryder bent down to pick up a shattered spindle and tossed it toward the rest of the trash. The move was smooth, casual—like taking a snap and tossing a football back in his high school days. And while every feminine instinct inside Lindsay sighed in appreciation at the way the worn denim molded to his perfect backside and muscular thighs, she refused to be distracted.

"According to Mrs. Webber, it was more than a broken pipe. She made it sound like the Great Flood."

"There was some water damage," he admitted.

Serious water damage from what Lindsay had been told. The pipe had broken a few weeks before Christmas, when Mrs. Webber's entire extended family was coming to spend the holiday at her house. Ryder had repaired the dry-wall, replaced the baseboards and refinished the wooden floors in record time.

"Mrs. Webber told me you worked almost around the clock to get everything done and yet somehow those extra hours never ended up on her bill."

Ryder's typical grin was fully back in place as he glanced over his shoulder. "Hell, Lindsay, you know I never was any good at math. Probably forgot to carry the one or something."

"Or something," she agreed, a little warily. She didn't believe for a second that he'd made an error. But she was having a hard time reconciling the man who would care enough about an old woman to work for free with the boy who, well, had cared only about himself.

"Good thing you'll be around to keep an eye on me for your grandmother's job. That's assuming you're ready to put your money where your mouth is."

"Excuse me?"

"If you're gonna be out here where the real work takes place, you'll have to be prepared to get dirty." His green gaze swept over her from head to toe, and Lindsay felt as if the nerves in her body had suddenly turned into Fourth of July sparklers. "Are you ready for that?"

Ready for the jumpy, excited, out-of-control way he made her feel? Not in this lifetime. But somehow she still couldn't resist one of Ryder's dares. "You're not going to scare me off, Kincaid."

"All right, then, but you'll have to change. Or maybe go shopping. Somehow I doubt you have any clothes that you wouldn't mind getting covered in sawdust and grit or splattered with paint."

"I'm not going to go out and buy a new outfit for that. I have something I can wear." Maybe she could borrow some of Ellie's gardening clothes and Ryder would never need to know. "I'm not afraid of hard work."

"Okay, Brookes. Show me what you've got." His grin broadened even further. "Can't wait to see you in a hard hat."

A hard hat? Lindsay hated wearing hats—even cute, fashionable ones. "Is that necessary?"

"Probably not. But I bet you'd look hot in one."

Chapter Six

A few days later, Lindsay didn't have any doubt that she looked hot. Unfortunately not in the way Ryder had insinuated. Despite the mild weather, the faded red T-shirt and khaki capris she'd borrowed from her grandmother clung to her and sweat trickled uncomfortably between her breasts. And that wasn't the worst of it. Wiping her forehead, she cringed at the feel of the sawdust that clung to every inch of her damp skin and seemed to have seeped into every pore, as well.

"I don't see why we have to sand the door if we're going to end up painting it anyway," she protested as she turned off the electric machine, still feeling the vibrations trembling in her hands and arms even with the motor off. She pulled off the worn piece of paper and installed a new, cut-to-fit sheet, something she was proud to have learned despite her complaints.

Not that she was about to tell Ryder about her sense of accomplishment over the small feat. Not when he seemed to own and know how to operate every power tool imaginable.

He glanced at the two sawhorses he'd set up to hold the front door so she wouldn't have to bend over on the ground. He, too, was covered head to toe with sawdust from working on the front porch with an upright floor sander much bigger than the handheld model she controlled. Somehow, though, the sweaty, disheveled look on him made her mouth as dry as, well, sawdust. And when he lifted the edge of his T-shirt to wipe his forehead, she wasn't sure she'd ever manage to swallow again.

The brief glimpse of tanned skin and hard-packed abs sent heat pooling low in her belly, and she leaned a hand against the door as her knees went weak. Luckily the solid wood was balanced well enough not to flip right up and smack her in the face, though that was probably what she deserved for lusting over Ryder Kincaid.

"Neither did your grandfather," he said, not unkindly, "which is why the door ended up looking the way it did."

Jumping down from the porch, which no longer had a set of front steps, as he'd pulled the rotting, warped boards off the day before, he strolled over to her side. Lindsay's heartbeat picked up its pace at his nearness, at the combination of fresh cut wood and a hint of pine-scent deodorant rising from his warm skin. He ran a hand over the section of pale wood she'd exposed, and goose bumps rose across her arms and chest as if he'd trailed that same hand over her naked skin.

"I know it's tempting to rush things. To jump right into the real action," he murmured as his palm lifted until only the brush of his fingertips followed the grain of the wood. "But in the end, that's never as…satisfying as taking your time, doing it right."

"No need to hurry… We have all night."

He'd taken his time their one night together, too. When

Lindsay would have rushed, eagerness and embarrassment combining into clumsy urgency, he'd slowed her down. Innocent and in love, Lindsay had cared about nothing but finally being in Ryder's arms. If only she'd known that one night would be their only night...

"That's something I've learned over the years."

Oh, yes, Lindsay could imagine the things he'd learned. "Ryder—"

"Here, Mom!"

Lindsay took a shaky step back as Robbie's voice cut through the air, slicing through the sexual tension and breaking the moment.

"I've got more sandpaper for you," he said as he rushed over. He stopped short with the cut sheets of paper—the job Ryder had assigned him—hanging from one hand. "Why are you guys standing around?"

"We were— I was...waiting for you to bring more paper." Ignoring the knowing look in Ryder's eyes as she took a brand-new piece of sandpaper to replace the one she hadn't used yet, she suggested, "I think it's time for a lunch break, don't you?"

Robbie nodded but gave the adults a quick look-over. "But Gran's never gonna let you in the house like that."

Ryder slapped his hand against his jeans, releasing a puff of sawdust. "You're probably right, but if you could bring some chairs outside, we've got a perfectly good table right here."

"You mean we're going to eat lunch on the front door?" Robbie giggled.

"Why not?"

They made a picnic out of it with all of them, including her grandmother, gathered around the outdoor "table" for turkey sandwiches, pasta salad and potato chips. "This is cool! We should eat like this all the time."

"I couldn't agree more, Robbie," Ellie said as she lifted her plastic cup of iced tea to tap against his milk.

It was on Lindsay's tongue to remind her grandmother that they could have family picnics together far more often once Ellie agreed to move to Phoenix, but she held silent. The meal had been filled with so much teasing and laughter that she didn't want to ruin the moment.

And it wouldn't be the same, not without Ryder.

The alfresco dining had been his idea, but more than that, he'd been the one to pull out Ellie's and Lindsay's chairs as if they were at a high-class restaurant. He'd been the one to explain with such enthusiasm the work they were doing that her grandmother's shock at seeing the torn-up front porch eased into a sense of excitement as she announced she couldn't wait to see the finished product. More often than not, Ryder had been the one making Ellie and Robbie laugh.

He'd always had such an easy way with people. All he had to do was turn on the Kincaid charm.

And Lindsay was anything but immune. Despite the tension-filled moment earlier, a moment that should have sent her running, Ryder had treated her the same as Robbie and Ellie during the meal, his smiles for her just as friendly and relaxed. It was enough to make her feel, well, anything but friendly and relaxed.

She hadn't simply…imagined that moment, had she? The suggestion in his voice? The heat in his gaze? Projecting her own lingering attraction for Ryder into his words and actions and seeing only want she wanted to see?

It was enough to make her want to crawl beneath their temporary table and hide.

"Are you all right, Lindsay? You look worried," Ellie said.

"I'm, um…" Worried? She supposed that was better than looking as though she was dying of embarrassment.

"I was wondering what happens next. After the front porch is finished."

Lindsay didn't know if the explanation worked for her grandmother, but it was enough for Ryder to pick up the conversation. "We'll stay outside for now and work on the brick path to the front steps," he said with a nod toward the walkway. The three-foot-wide section cut through the grass in a curving arc toward the porch, but the bricks had sunk in some spots and heaved in others, creating a path that was anything but smooth.

"We'll dig out more of the ground beneath the bricks, spread a decomposed granite base and use a compactor to pack it down. Then we'll reuse the bricks your husband picked out," he said to Ellie. "He had a great idea with that walkway, and when it's done, I hope it'll look like it did when he first laid it."

Ellie's eyes glistened behind her glasses as she reached across the table to place her hand on Ryder's. "Thank you."

Ellie wasn't simply talking about fixing the pathway, and Lindsay's throat ached at Ryder's thoughtfulness. Using the same bricks and following the same path her grandfather had laid would help keep Robert Brookes's memory alive in the house he and her grandmother loved. Even though Lindsay and Ryder had discussed how important that was to Ellie, he'd still surprised her by taking her words so much to heart.

"All I'm looking for is a chance to prove I'm not the same guy I was in high school."

Only a few days ago, Lindsay had questioned whether or not Ryder would be able to convince her. But now a bigger question loomed like dark clouds of the summer monsoons that rolled across the valley back home. Had Lindsay changed enough from the girl *she'd* been in high school?

Did she have the courage to do now what she hadn't done back then? Could she tell Ryder that he was Robbie's father?

"I don't know, Bryce," Ryder hedged as he tucked the cell phone against his shoulder and walked a few yards away from Lindsay and her family. He'd been dodging his brother's texts the past few days, shooting back vague responses, knowing Bryce wouldn't be put off for much longer. Ryder could have ducked this call as well, but while the texts made it clear nothing was wrong, he didn't want to risk sending a call that could have been important to voice mail. As it turned out, he'd have been better off not answering.

"I've got this big remodeling job going on for Ellie Brookes. I'm refinishing the porch, and I want to get the new front steps finished—"

"The barbecue's not until tonight. You know—Friday night? As in after work? Besides, you told me yourself that you were starting with the exterior of the house. Once the sun starts going down, how much could you really get done? And why exactly are you avoiding a family barbecue anyway?"

"I'm not avoiding it. You know I'm always front and center whenever the family gets together."

"Yeah, you always are…except for now when you've been blowing off my texts and are telling me you have to work." His voice turning more serious, Bryce said, "Come on, Ry… What's going on?"

Before he could answer, Lindsay called out, "Ryder, do you want dessert? It's strawberry—" She put a hand to her mouth as he turned and she spotted the phone against his ear. "Sorry," she whispered as she backed away.

The midday sun gleamed in the golden highlights streaked through her hair. She'd caught the shoulder-length locks back into a high ponytail that made her look like a teenager. Only she'd never pulled her hair back when they were in high school. Instead she'd worn her long hair like a shield, lowering her head and ducking behind the caramel-brown curtain whenever anyone made eye contact.

She'd surprised him over the past few days by not backing down from the remodeling work. Not that Ryder had questioned her willingness to work hard. He'd always admired her determination. No B-pluses for Lindsay Brookes. Only straight A's would do. But rolling up her sleeves and getting dirty? That he hadn't expected.

Any more than he had expected to find it such a turn-on...

"Ryder—Ry, are you still there?"

Ryder jerked his gaze away from Lindsay's retreating figure to refocus on his brother yelling in his ear. "Yeah, yeah, I'm still here."

"Is that the reason you don't want to come over to the house tonight?" Amusement filled Bryce's voice, but Ryder felt he'd missed the joke.

"Is what the reason?"

"Lindsay 'Book-Brain' Brookes... That was her, wasn't it, offering you *dessert*?"

"Yeah, offering me dessert that we'll be eating right alongside her grandmother and young son, so get your mind out of the gutter."

Strawberry, Lindsay had started to say. Cheesecake? Ice cream? Pie? Ryder would have said yes to any of the above, but more than that, he'd like to taste the summer-fresh fruit right from Lindsay's lips. Lips that were the color of ripe strawberries and far more tempting...

"If the two of you have something going on—"

"I didn't say that," Ryder protested. Which wasn't the same as saying he didn't wish he and Lindsay had something going on.

"Then there's no reason for you not to come to the barbecue tonight."

Ryder swallowed a frustrated sigh. No reason other than the barbecue would be the perfect opportunity for Bryce and Nina to announce to friends and family that they were expecting. "Look, Bryce—"

"Why not invite them along?"

"What?"

"Lindsay and her son. Heck, even her grandmother."

Invite them along... Suddenly the thought of the barbecue didn't seem like such a bad idea. This would be a chance for Robbie to hang out with some kids right around his own age. As a lifelong Clearville resident, Ellie would likely know several people there. And Lindsay—

He wanted Lindsay there. Wanted the chance to spend more time with her without her son and grandmother right underfoot. Of course, if he invited her to the barbecue, his family would also be in the way, but if this gathering was like the others his brother had had, it would be quite a crowd. And sometimes it was easy getting lost in a crowd...

"I'll think about it," Ryder said, knowing the words were true. He'd be thinking of little else now that his brother had planted the idea in his head.

"I expect you to be there," Bryce warned. "And if you're not, the next family gathering's going to be at your house."

Ryder groaned, imagining his family and half the neighborhood showing up unexpectedly at his bachelor pad with its sparse furnishings and mostly empty fridge. He'd never hear the end of it and wouldn't put it past his brother to do as he'd threatened.

"I'll be there, all right? Enough with the arm twisting."

Ryder disconnected the call and slid the phone into his pocket. Lindsay had wandered back to the table, where she was clearing away the paper plates and napkins from their lunch. Ellie must have gone back to the kitchen for the strawberry dessert with Robbie at her heels. Probably hoping to sneak an extra serving away from his mother's watchful eye.

"Everything okay?" she asked as he joined. He grabbed the garbage bag and held it open while she tossed everything inside.

"Yeah. Why?"

She lifted a shoulder in a shrug that had a small smile curving his lips, the gesture so reminiscent of Robbie's frequent response. "When you were on the phone—not that I heard anything," she pointed out quickly. "But from the look on your face, you seemed...upset."

Ryder fought back a curse. And that right there was why he didn't want to go to the barbecue. If Lindsay had picked up on his expression from across the yard, how was he supposed to hide his feelings when he was up close and personal with his family?

"It's...nothing."

"Oh, okay. Sure." Her movements were as jerky as her words as she tossed the last of the used flatware in the trash. "Well, I should go check on dessert."

He caught her arm before she could turn away. "Lindsay..."

Her movements slowed, her stance softening slightly, as she met his gaze. "It's okay, Ryder. You don't have to tell me. I mean, it's not like we're best friends or anything."

She said the words with a light laugh, but it wasn't enough to soften the blow. And yet Ryder was surprised to find the words packed a punch. "Maybe not now, but we were friends once, Lindsay. Back in high school, I told you things I never told anyone else."

A slight blush lit her face as she glanced away only to bring her blue-green gaze back to his again. "That's not true. Is it?"

"Hell, yeah. I never would have admitted to Brittany or any of my friends on the team that I'd get so nervous before a big game I'd make myself sick. My teammates would have laughed it off, and Brittany's response wouldn't have been much better. But you understood back then." Ryder sucked in a deep breath. "Just like you'll probably understand now when… My brother and sister-in-law found out they're expecting another child."

And as she had in high school, Lindsay searched his expression, seeing past the words and straight through to everything he wasn't saying. "The news caught you off guard, didn't it?"

"It shouldn't have. I mean, Bryce and Nina are great parents, so why wouldn't they want to have another child? They're the perfect family, the perfect couple."

"No relationship is perfect all the time."

His sure as hell hadn't been. But he didn't want to talk about Brittany right now. Not with Lindsay standing close enough for him to catch the sun-warmed scent of her skin. Close enough for him to reach out and free her hair from her ponytail if he dared. Close enough for him to remember how it felt to kiss her and to make him wonder what life might have been like if that night in high school had been the start of something instead of the end and if Lindsay's coming back to town might give them a second chance…

"So, you and— You wanted kids?"

Lindsay's hesitant question snapped him out of his daydream like a shot of ice water in the face. Kids. Yeah, he'd wanted kids, but Brittany… He swallowed against the burning in his gut as he gruffly said, "I wanted to start a family."

"Oh, I didn't— I guess I never realized…" Her voice was small, soft, the rest of her words brushed away by a wisp of a sigh.

Was she thinking of her own hopes and dreams of a

family? Ryder had heard the rumors, juicy gossip Brittany had eagerly passed along, but he'd never heard the whole story of what had happened with Lindsay and Tony Pirelli all those years ago. Had she hoped Tony would marry her when she got pregnant with Robbie? Had she thought the three of them might be a family?

"Life doesn't always turn out the way you plan, does it? But some things aren't mean to be, and now I get to be the favorite uncle," he joked.

Lindsay swallowed before matching his fake smile with one of her own. "Let me guess," she added, "you're the only uncle."

"Yep. All aunts on Nina's side of the family." One of whom was single and would undoubtedly be at the barbecue that evening. The uncomfortable thought prompted him to blurt out, "We're having a get-together over at my brother's house tonight. You should come."

Her gaze widened in surprise. "I should—what?"

"Come with me tonight as my guest."

"Oh, I don't think so, Ryder. You said it was a family thing."

"Friends, family, half the neighborhood's probably invited. You can bring Robbie. It'll give him a chance to get to know some kids. Ellie, too, if she's up to it."

"Gran loves to socialize," Lindsay admitted almost reluctantly. "She's never met a stranger."

Ryder smiled. "I'm taking that as a yes, and I'll pick you all up around six."

Chapter Seven

As Ryder led the way around his brother's house, across a lush front lawn to a side gate, the sound of kids and laughter grew louder with each step. So, too, did the voice in Lindsay's head.

This was a mistake. I never should have agreed to this!

As if sensing some of his mother's reservations, or perhaps suffering from his own, Robbie hesitated as Ryder opened the back gate to an expansive yard. Green grass stretched toward a tree line a hundred feet from the back of the house, and clusters of people gathered throughout.

Women milled around two picnic tables, carrying and arranging platters of food—sides and desserts to go with the mouthwatering scent of burgers and dogs sizzling on the grill. A few men had gathered around the state-of-the-art, stainless steel barbecue that took center stage in an outdoor kitchen complete with a rock-face bar and granite countertop.

A burst of laughter followed a loud pop and hiss as some

grease dripped into the fire. The sound caught the attention of another group of men and women on the far side of the yard, playing a game of touch football.

"Try not to burn them all to a crisp!" one of the men yelled out to the brown-haired man who held up a pair of tongs in a subtly offensive gesture, drawing another laugh from the crowd.

"Bryce," a pretty brunette chided from the food table. "Mind your manners in front of our guests."

"What guests?" he called back. "These are all our friends!"

"Okay, in front of the children, then."

The man's eyes glowed as the woman lightly touched her stomach, and Lindsay realized the couple had to be Ryder's brother and sister-in-law. And speaking of children, they seemed to be everywhere. Darting in and round the food table, dodging light slaps on the hand as they tried to sneak a dessert or two before dinner. Giving the adults a run for their money in the football game. Waving their hands in front of their faces and choking with great exaggeration as the smoke from the grill drifted their way. And Robbie dropped another step back as the adults made their way through the gate.

"Look at all the kids, Robbie," Ellie announced. "Why don't you head on over and say hi?"

Lindsay's heart broke a little as her son adamantly shook his head. She hated that it was so hard for him to break out of his shell, to make friends, to show his peers what a smart and funny kid he was.

This had been a mistake, and not for the reasons Lindsay had originally feared. A hot wash of shame swept over her that she had been so focused on her own concerns she'd lost sight of her son's. "Maybe this wasn't such a good idea. We should—"

"It's okay, Lindsay," Ryder reassured her. "I know it

looks like a rowdy bunch back here, but trust me, we don't bite."

And then he winked, and heaven help her if she didn't feel a small, seductive thrill straight from her head to her toes and every place in between.

"And hey, Rob, you've been such a big helper to me these past few days at your gran's house, I was thinking maybe you could help me out tonight, too."

Looking curious despite himself, Robbie slowly asked, "How?"

"Well, see, my brother's family has this great dog named Cowboy. He's a border collie, so he's supersmart, knows all these tricks and loves kids. But the thing is, he gets a little nervous around a big group of people like this, and so my brother usually keeps him in the house..."

Ryder's shoulders lifted on a big sigh as he knelt down in front of Robbie. "He's all alone in there, and I think, even though he gets a little scared, he'd much rather be out here. Maybe if you could kinda keep an eye on him and hang out with him, then he wouldn't be so afraid. What do you think?"

"I like dogs... Do you really think I could help him not be so scared?"

"I know you could, Robbie." Certainty filled Ryder's voice, and the little boy's chest puffed out at the vote of confidence. "So why don't we go get Cowboy?"

"All right!"

He'd already started to rush ahead when Lindsay called out, "Robbie, wait!"

He and Ryder turned to face her, Ryder holding the gate open and Robbie poised and ready to rush on through, both with a questioning look on their faces. The quirk of a right eyebrow, the wrinkle across the forehead... Was it only her imagination or were Ryder and Robbie starting to look more and more alike?

Her throat swelled with all Ryder was trying to do, and she had to swallow hard to get the words out. "I need to talk to Ryder for a minute first."

Her son's shoulders instantly dropped—already anticipating what she might say?—and he whined out a protest, "Aw, Mom!"

"Just for a minute." She caught Ryder's gaze as she stepped away from her disgruntled son. "I know you're trying to ease Robbie out of his shell, and I appreciate it." Such a bland word for the rush of emotion bubbling inside her at the kind and thoughtful way he treated her son. Not pushing or forcing Robbie into the situation *for his own good*—as many adults had when *she* had been the shy, socially inept child—but instead touching on an opportunity for Robbie to find his own way out of the self-conscious cocoon.

"He's a great kid, Lindsay."

Sincerity shone in Ryder's green eyes, and she fought not to flinch as his words sent an arrow straight to her heart.

Oh, Ryder. He's so much more than a great kid. He's a great son.

And like earlier in the day when he'd confessed that he wanted children, that he wanted a family, the truth beat so hard against her chest, she half expected the words to break free.

But then the same fear that had lingered in her heart for the past decade whispered through her mind. *He wanted to have a child with Brittany, to start a family with Brittany. He never said he wanted one with* you.

She'd believed Ryder once when he told her he wanted her. Believed that one night was the beginning of a bright and brilliant future where the two of them were a couple, where they were in love...

Instead that night had been the beginning and the end.

A few days later, Ryder had gone back to Brittany. To the girl he truly wanted, the girl he truly loved.

"Hey, everything okay?" Ryder asked as her "just a minute" had clearly stretched on too long without her saying a word. He reached out and palmed her upper arm. A friendly, concerned gesture, nothing more, and yet pinpricks of awareness spread in all directions—down to her tingling fingertips, across her collarbone and down to her breasts.

Lindsay longed to lean into his touch, to breach the small distance between them. The summer breeze shifted away from the smoke and charcoal of the grill to tease her with the even more mouthwatering scent of minty soap, laundry detergent and…Ryder.

"I know you're trying to help, but putting Robbie in charge of Cowboy might not be the best idea. I'm sure he's a great dog, but if he does get nervous or scared…well, he's still an animal and there's no telling how he might react."

Ryder's eyes crinkled as he held back a smile, and the slight pressure on her arm increased as he gave a bone-melting squeeze. "I may have…overstated Cowboy's fear of crowds," he murmured, keeping his voice low enough so Robbie couldn't overhear.

"So, he's not afraid?"

"Cowboy's a border collie mix. He lives for crowds. Adventure and excitement could be his middle name, although Nina will tell you it's Trouble. If they let him out of the house, he'll try herding all the kids or playing keep-away with the plastic football or sneaking food from the table and grill every few minutes. That dog has as much energy as he has smarts, and it pretty much takes the whole family to keep up with him. But," Ryder added when Lindsay would have voiced another protest, "he's also leash-trained. As long as Robbie keeps hold of him and pays attention to him—like I know he will—Cowboy will behave. I promise."

The mix of boyish sincerity and masculine confidence chipped away at her defenses until Lindsay couldn't squash the smile tugging at her lips. "You promise, huh?"

"That Cowboy will behave? Yep." A devilish twinkle sparked in his eyes as he added, "That I will?" He shook his head. "No guarantees there."

"Planning on stealing some food off the grill?"

That tempting gaze dropped to her lips as he murmured, "I was thinking of something a little sweeter."

Lindsay's heart stuttered inside her chest even as warning lights flashed through her mind. A misbehaving Ryder Kincaid was the last thing she needed. Even on his best behavior, he was more than she could handle!

Giving him a playful shove in the shoulder, she said, "Go get Cowboy, will you?"

Overhearing her, Robbie exclaimed, "All right! Thanks, Mom!"

The two guys exchanged a quick high five before striding toward the house, and Lindsay tried to pretend she hadn't noticed the similarities in the triumphant grins they'd shot at her...

"The boy will be fine, Lindsay," her grandmother chimed in as she looked around the crowded yard with interest. "Clearville's always been a wonderful place for children. Remember how you loved growing up here."

She had loved it as a child. Too many of her memories were focused on her teenage years—the growing pains and heartache of high school—that she'd forgot about the earlier days and the freedom of running through the neighborhoods and town. Safe and secure in a place where everyone knew everyone else and looked out for each other. "You're right, Gran. I did love growing up here."

Ellie offered a pleased smile and a small nod. "I knew

it," she murmured. "Oh, look! There's Sharon Elsworth. She recommended a fascinating murder-mystery novel to me the last time I saw her. I've been meaning to talk to her about it. It was a great book...even if I did figure out whodunit before the end."

And with that, her grandmother was off to cross the lawn to where the fifty-something school librarian stood near the cooler, handing out ice-cold sodas and keeping an eye on the teenagers in case they thought to grab one of the beers instead.

Lindsay heard the squeak of a hinge and the slap of the screen door slamming shut over the other sounds of the party and turned in time to see Robbie leading a medium-sized black-and-white dog down the back porch steps. She had to smile a little at the sight. Between the dog's expressive face and its bright blue eyes—not to mention the red bandanna tied around his neck—the name Cowboy fit.

Her breath caught for a second when the dog tugged, pulling the leash and Robbie's arm straight out from his body, afraid he was about to tumble right down the steps. But Ryder was right there, bracing a hand on Robbie's shoulder and showing him how to keep the dog at his side.

Reaching the thick, lush grass, Ryder continued the lesson with both boy and dog watching him with eager, attentive gazes. After only a few minutes, and a pocketful of treats, Ryder had instructed Robbie how to command the dog to sit, stay, lie down, roll over and come with nothing more than half a dozen or so hand gestures.

And her son was loving every minute of it.

Before long, Ryder left Robbie to handle Cowboy on his own like a seasoned pro, and his smile was more than a little smug as he sauntered back over to her. "One well-behaved dog and one happy kid, as promised."

Robbie bent down to shake Cowboy's paw, and a smile tugged at her lips despite her concerns. "You were right."

Ryder took a staggering step backward. "Words I never thought I'd hear you say."

"Very funny."

"So, where's Ellie?"

"Over with Sharon Elsworth."

"The high school librarian?" Catching sight of the two older women, he leaned close to murmur, "Remember when she caught us together in the stacks?"

"Caught us…" Heat prickled beneath her skin at the innuendo in his voice. "You make it sound like we were trying to get away with something."

Even she'd been aware that couples had tried sneaking off to the back of the library to steal a few moments of hormone-driven privacy.

That was not why she and Ryder had hidden out back there.

"We were," Ryder argued. "Or at least I was. Last thing I wanted was for my teammates to know you were tutoring me in calculus."

"I still don't know why you were worried. Most of the guys on the team didn't even bother to take calculus."

"Exactly. A far as they were concerned, I was already an egghead for getting B's. If they knew I was actually getting tutored, they never would have let me live it down. Embarrassment alone would have killed me," he said with a smile that flashed perfect white teeth and a hint of dimple beneath the five o'clock shadow he hadn't shaved away.

The combination was enough to send a surge of heat pooling low in her belly. He was every bit the confident man; it was hard to believe he'd ever been an insecure teenager. He'd had it all. Star quarterback, team captain, prom king and half of Clearville High's perfect couple. "It really would have bothered you if your friends had known I was tutoring you?"

"Back then?" He shrugged. "Sure. Why? What did you think I was doing hiding out in the stacks with you?"

Honestly, she'd thought he was worried about being seen with her—a geeky book-brain so far removed from the "cool" crowd. Had he hid his fears so well or had her own self-consciousness blinded her to anything beyond her own insecurity?

Lindsay shook her head. "It…it doesn't matter now. High school was a long time ago."

"Yeah, it was." His gaze locked on to hers as he searched her expression. "Long enough, maybe, that we might have a chance to start over?"

Ryder had any number of reasons not to kiss Lindsay. Their awkward past, his more recent divorce, not to mention her grandmother and son and practically his whole family a few yards away.

All good, sound reasons not to kiss her, but none of them enough to make the desire go away. And when his gaze fell to her lips just inches away, the need reflected in her expression added to his.

"Ryder…" Her husky whisper drew him closer, close enough for him to catch a hint of her summer-fresh scent, close enough for him to feel the brush of her warm breath against his skin.

He heard his name again. Not in the low vibration that reached inside and grabbed hold of his guts, but in a high-pitched, perky chirp that had him cringing instead.

Lindsay had jumped back at the sound, and Ryder turned to see his sister-in-law Jessie jogging toward them.

Her reddish-blond hair was caught up in a high ponytail that swayed in time with each step she took. Her long legs and arms were left bare by a skimpy white tank top and red shorts that did more to highlight her curves than hide them. Not long ago, Nina's baby sister had been a skinny, freckle-faced preteenager. He couldn't help picturing that young girl whenever he saw Jessie any more than he could help thinking, *How the hell did that happen?*

"Hey, Jessie."

"I was hoping you'd—" Jessie stopped short when she caught sight of Lindsay at his side. "Oh, hi."

"Jessie, this is Lindsay. Lindsay, this is Nina's little sister."

A wry half smile tilted Jessie's lips as she pointed out, "Not so little anymore."

"Yeah, I know." And, man, if that didn't make him feel…old.

"So, how do you two know each other?"

"Lindsay and I went to high school together. We both moved away after graduation, and it's kind of like…fate, you know, that we're both back in town now. We've known each other a long time, haven't we, Lins?" He draped an arm over her shoulders, half expecting her to elbow him right in his ribs after the fulminating look she shot him from the corner of her eye.

"That's right, *Ry.*"

"Oh, well…" Jessie's gaze cut between the two of them, but she didn't give up easily. "We've got a game of touch football going if you want to join." Her ponytail swung over one should with the challenging toss of her head as she called back over her shoulder. "You can be on my team."

Ryder had no intention of playing any "touch" games with Jessie. Even if his brother wouldn't threaten to barbecue a few of his body parts on the grill if he got too close to Jessie, he was too old for her. Knowing her as well as he had when she was a kid made the whole idea seem a little…creepy. Not to mention that her encouraging glances didn't come close to affecting him the way a "you're dead meat" glare from Lindsay did.

"'Lins'?" she echoed with a questioning lift to one eyebrow.

"Sorry, I guess I went back in time for a minute or two."

"Well, that would explain the immature behavior."

"Hey, wait!" Ryder caught up with her as she stalked off toward the crowds gathered in the center of the yard. He'd expected her to be annoyed, but this… "Why are you so pissed off?"

"You're really going to ask me that after—" Jerking out of his grasp, she waved a dismissive hand. "Forget it. You know, I'd hoped you had changed, but you're the same guy you were in high school."

"What does Jessie have to do with high school?" What did *any* of this have to do with high school?

"Using me to make your girlfriend jealous? What, not ringing any bells?"

"That is not what I was doing. Not then and sure as hell not now!"

A burst of laughter from the women gathered around the picnic tables barely registered, but the sound was enough of a reminder. One of the reasons he'd invited Lindsay along was to keep his bad attitude from ruining the barbecue. Getting in a fight with her wasn't what he'd had in mind.

Ignoring her protest, he backed her through the gate and pulled her around to the back of Bryce's detached garage. The yard's wooden fence ran behind the structure, but the small gap between was a perfect hiding place when his young nephews were trying to avoid punishment. Too bad it wasn't just boys who could get themselves in trouble, Ryder thought, meeting Lindsay's flashing eyes as she jerked out of his grasp again.

"Jessie is not my girlfriend. Trying to make her jealous was the last thing on my mind. If anything, I thought her seeing me with you might make her realize I'm not interested."

Lindsay's rigid posture eased slightly, her shoulders lowering, the arms she'd crossed beneath her breasts loosening. "Why wouldn't you be interested? She's a beautiful girl."

"'Girl' is right. She's too young. And even if she wasn't, she's family. Maybe not by blood, but still close enough to be seriously messy."

And he'd had enough of seriously messy after six years spent working with his in-laws.

He'd known the minute he stepped foot inside Baines and Associates that he was making a mistake. Yes, he'd obtained a degree in architecture, and yes, he loved the idea of creating something out of nothing, of watching an entirely new building take shape on a computer screen. But he wanted to work for himself, willing to start small and struggle through those first lean years.

Brittany hadn't understood.

"It's my grandfather's company," she'd argued. "You know he wants you to work for him. It only makes sense to keep the business in the family."

But he'd learned a lot in college—some while sitting in classrooms and lecture halls, but the most important lessons in the time he'd spent riding the bench during the football season. Success, he'd realized, didn't always come easy and the hardest-fought victories always tasted the sweetest.

"I want to earn my own place," he'd argued.

"You will," Brittany promised.

But all he'd earned was resentment from his peers and a lack of respect from his bosses as he'd been trotted out as a company figurehead, the poster boy for groundbreaking ceremonies and ribbon cutting at grand openings. And the whole experience had left him with nothing but a bitter aftertaste in his mouth.

But even if he hadn't been burned by mixing business

and pleasure, family and business, none of that really mattered.

Because it wasn't Jessie he was interested in.

Lindsay's mouth twisted as she gave a scoffing laugh. "Seriously messy? Kind of like sleeping with me while you were still dating Brittany?"

Of course, it also wasn't Jessie who thought the worst of him. Who still blamed him for something that had happened ten years ago. And maybe it was what he deserved, but he couldn't pretend Lindsay's accusations hadn't hurt.

A hell of a lot less than the hurt you caused her.

"I wasn't seeing her. Not…then. We'd broken up, for good, I'd thought." And he'd wondered, over the years, what life might have been like if they'd stayed broken up. If that one night with Lindsay had been one to remember instead of a night guilt and regret urged him to forget.

"I never meant to hurt you, Lindsay, and I'm sorry. If I could go back in time and change things—"

"You can't." Exhaling with a sigh, she dropped her arms, lowering the last of her defenses. Looking up, she met his gaze, and the mix of emotions in her blue-green eyes—the sadness and vulnerability—was another blow to his gut. "And I wouldn't."

"Wouldn't?"

"Wouldn't change things. What happened…" Her shoulders rose and fell with a shrug. "Happened."

"That doesn't mean I can't wish I'd done things differently."

Given the chance, he'd do everything differently. He'd want a big, luxurious bed to lay Lindsay down on instead of the cramped backseat of his car. He'd slowly strip the clothes from her body, revealing all that smooth skin and those delicate curves inch by inch rather than fumbling through and beneath fabric. He'd spend an eternity longer kissing the parted lips mere inches from his own rather than rushing to the finish line.

They weren't kids anymore. Lindsay had a confidence, a maturity and a strength that had been missing in high school. Qualities almost as attractive as the womanly curves that drew his eye as she sucked in a quick breath.

All of it different. All of it that much more tempting.

She looked gorgeous in a pale yellow sundress with white daisies embroidered on the hem. The halter-style bodice left her shoulders and arms bare, hugged the delicate swell of her breasts and narrow waist before flaring, bell-like, to her knees. Another woman might have come across as overdressed for a backyard barbecue, but Lindsay looked perfect.

Almost too perfect. Like some fancy dessert too beautiful to touch, but what good was food if you couldn't eat it? And the sweetest things in life were made to be tasted…

Lindsay's soft start of surprise vibrated against his lips as he covered her mouth with his own. Had he met with the slightest resistance, he would have stopped. But at the first touch, she opened to his kiss, the hands she'd braced on his chest fisting in his T-shirt and drawing him closer.

The dessert she'd offered after lunch had been homemade strawberry ice cream. The cold, creamy treat had melted on his tongue, summer fresh but still with the slightest tang. Sweet…but not too sweet.

It was a flavor he savored in Lindsay's kiss. Soft and sweet but with a bite that had him coming back for more.

The halter dress left her back bare, her skin silky smooth beneath his palm. And when his fingers brushed the tie at her neck, the awareness that a single tug would bare her breasts to his hungry gaze left him light-headed. Their softness pressed against his chest, the hard points of her nipples teasing him, and the hand he'd slid down to her hips instinctively tightened. Pulling her closer to the hardness of his own body and tempting them both.

Lindsay groaned, a sound of giving voice to the need spiraling out of control between them. And as the kiss deepened—drugging desire pulling them closer to the edge and into a seductive, sensual place where only the two of them existed a world away from the burgers grilling on the barbecue, away from the talking and laughter on the other side of the fence, away from the curious gazes and speculation of his friends and family—the tension teetered on a breaking point. A moment where Ryder wouldn't be able to stop himself from taking things further than he should. A moment where Lindsay broke off the kiss with a gasp, ducked beneath his arm and raced away.

Chapter Eight

The grass growing behind the detached garage was long and damp. The blades caught at her sandaled feet and bare ankles almost as if trying to hold her back, but Lindsay quickened her pace.

There had been plenty of times in her life when she'd been a coward. When she'd faced the plus sign on the pregnancy test. When she'd spent the next few months doing her best to hide that pregnancy. When she'd refused to tell her parents who the father of her child was and when she'd gone along with Tony's idea to allow them—and the rest of Clearville—to believe he was the boy responsible.

She'd admit to being terrified in each and every one of those instances, and she'd let that fear rule her actions.

But running away from Ryder now, that wasn't a matter of cowardice. That was about...survival.

"That doesn't mean I don't wish I could do things differently..."

And oh, how she'd wanted him to do those things. The

same, different, none of it mattered to the longing that had raced through her veins at the desire written in his gaze. Not so long as it meant Ryder kissing her, holding her, making love to her again and again and again…

Bursting out from behind the garage, Lindsay looked toward the vehicles haphazardly parked in front of the house. Had she brought her own and had Ellie and Robbie not still been in the backyard, part of the party going on without her and Ryder, Lindsay would have jumped into her car and raced away. Likely not stopping until she reached Phoenix.

But she didn't have her car, and she didn't have her grandmother or her son with her, so she wasn't going anywhere…except back to the barbecue.

Sucking in a deep breath, Lindsay opened the gate and stepped inside. The same people were gathered around the grill, the tables, the expanse of lawn. Everyone laughing and having a good time. Her legs were still trembling, her heart was still racing and her throat was still dry, all from that brief moment with Ryder. But as she eyed the various groups, a cold chill washed over her.

How many times had she stood just like this, frozen in place be it on the bus, in the cafeteria, in study hall, longing to find a place where she belonged, a table where she'd be welcomed instead of ignored?

This isn't high school. You're not that same shy girl.

Moving to Phoenix after graduation, she'd forced herself to leave that part of herself behind. She was going to be a single mother, and if she wanted to be a successful single mother, someone her child could be proud of, she had to find a way to break out of the insecure shell that had always surrounded her and to face the world with her head held high.

It hadn't been easy, and many times she'd wanted nothing more than to retreat into that familiar cocoon. But whenever she felt the fear start to take over, she forced herself to face it.

Instead of taking English classes in college and losing herself in the comforting, make-believe world of fiction, she'd signed up for courses in marketing, in public relations. She'd joined the debate team. Had she been afraid of heights, her college curriculum would have been comparable to walking on a tightrope a hundred feet above the ground.

And despite what she might have initially thought, her shyness was not terminal. She'd survived, and more than that, she'd thrived—both during college and in the career that followed.

So how had a few days in her hometown turned back the clock ten years? How had she reverted to that same shy girl she'd once been?

And how had one kiss from Ryder made her feel that she could fall for him all over again?

Not happening. She wouldn't—couldn't—fall for him again.

Setting her shoulders, she walked over to one of the tables nearly groaning under the mouthwatering spread of food. The brunette she'd recognized earlier as Ryder's sister-in-law was arranging paper plates and plastic utensils and humming what Lindsay recognized as a lullaby beneath her breath.

"Hi, you must be Nina. I'm Lindsay."

"Lindsay!" The other woman's eyes brightened. "So nice to meet you." Nodding toward the expansive lawn, she said, "I understand the dog lover is your son?"

"Yes, that's Robbie."

A bit of the tension eased from her spine as she watched Robbie putting the border collie through its paces. Ryder had been so good with him, and that was what she wanted, wasn't it? For Robbie and Ryder to have the chance to get to know each other before she revealed they were father and son? Now she just needed to find a way to keep her distance even as the two of them grew closer.

"Bryce said that you and Ryder went to school together?"

"Yes, we graduated in the same class, and then I moved away with my parents right after that."

"So, are you back for the reunion?"

She'd almost forgotten about the upcoming event. Or more likely *tried* to forget, ignoring the emails and Facebook posts counting down the days until the big night. "Um, no. I'm not planning on going."

"That's too bad. Ryder says he's not, either. I thought maybe you could talk him into it."

"I'm surprised he doesn't want to go. Have the chance to relive his glory days."

Nina sighed. "I think that's part of the problem. Life doesn't always work out the way you think it will when you're eighteen, does it?"

Not for her, and not for Ryder, either.

Like so many of their classmates, Lindsay had been sure Ryder had a stellar college and professional football career ahead of him. She'd thought he had a future of fame and fortune. He was destined for bigger and better things, while her own dreams had seemed so much simpler and…smaller.

Never would she have imagined ten years later that they would both be back in their hometown.

"Do you need a hand with any of this?" she asked Nina, waving at the table.

"No, I think we're about ready to eat, and it looks like your grandmother wants to talk to you."

Lindsay glanced over to see Ellie waving her over to where she stood next to a woman who looked vaguely familiar. "Do you remember Patricia Bennett?" her grandmother asked as she walked over. "She's my good friend Barbara's niece."

"Yes, of course. Good to see you again."

Patricia smiled. "After talking with my aunt, I've been meaning to get in touch with you."

"You have?" She glanced over at her grandmother, who gazed back with a wide-eyed innocence that didn't fool Lindsay for a second.

"Aunt Barbara told me about your experience in public relations, and I really think you'd be the perfect fit."

"Fit for—"

"Isn't that wonderful, Lindsay?" Ellie interrupted. "The Clearville Chamber of Commerce has a job opening and could use someone like you."

Lindsay opened her mouth again, but this time Patricia jumped in before she could speak. "We all think Clearville's about the greatest town there is, but we have to be realistic. Many of the smaller farmers in the outlying communities are selling out as the previous generations are getting older and too many of the younger generation are moving on to bigger cities. We need to find ways to keep our young people—like you—here in town by increasing our visibility to tourists, promoting the businesses our town has to offer and increasing job opportunities."

"Patricia..." Lindsay began, and this time the other woman and her grandmother both remained silent, waiting to hear what she had to say. Only Lindsay didn't know where to start—with Patricia's mistaken impression that she was moving back to Clearville and looking for a job? With her grandmother, who'd undoubtedly given Patricia that impression? But instead the words that came out of her mouth were "What have you done so far?"

"Several of the local businesses have joined forces. Some new rental cabins have opened recently and the owner is working with one of the shops in town to decorate the interiors, and both businesses are promoting each other with flyers and on their websites. Hillcrest House is focusing on offering all-inclusive wedding packages, and they've contracted with the local bakery for their wedding cakes. But we're still interested in finding ways to expand on all of this. We could really use your expertise."

At that, Patricia paused and looked at Lindsay expectantly, as if she was waiting for her to spout out a dozen or so ideas to make the town flourish.

"It sounds like a great opportunity, but I already have a job back in Phoenix," Lindsay said with a pointed glance at her grandmother.

"Oh, I thought…" Patricia's confused frown told exactly what she'd thought, but Ellie was quick to jump in.

"You're here now. And there's no reason why you couldn't help out during your stay, is there?"

"I'm here to help you with the house, Gran."

But Ellie waved that protest aside. "We hired Ryder to fix the house. He doesn't need you watching over his every move."

Though Patricia tried to hide it, Lindsay could see the instant speculation sparking in the other woman's eyes.

"I wasn't watching Ryder," she lied. Flat-out, pants-on-fire lied to her grandmother. "I was watching out for my son, Robbie. He wants to 'help' with the remodeling," she explained to Patricia, "but I don't want him getting in the way or getting hurt."

"I can keep an eye on my own great-grandson for a few hours each day. Besides, I think Robbie's new friends will keep him plenty busy."

"His new…" Lindsay's voice trailed away as she followed her grandmother's gaze to the far side of the yard where Cowboy was now off-leash, a Frisbee in his mouth as he ran circles around a group of boys.

"Catch him, Rob!" one of the brown-haired boys called

out, and Robbie reached for the black-and-white streak of fur as the dog raced by. But the border collie dodged his grasp, and Robbie went sprawling face-first in the grass, his bangs flopping over his eyes and his glasses landing a few feet away.

Even from across the yard, Lindsay could tell her son wasn't hurt, but the pain of his embarrassment was palatable as he ducked his head and reached for his glasses. And when the other boys started to laugh...

Lindsay was halfway across the lawn when a warm hand caught her elbow, holding her back. She wasn't sure when Ryder had rejoined the barbecue, but she jerked against his hold.

"Give him a chance," Ryder said.

Every instinct within Lindsay rebelled. She wanted to race to her son's side, to protect him from all the hurts of the world—whether it was skinned knees or bruised pride. But the warmth of Ryder's touch, the encouragement in his voice, held her still. She watched, barely breathing, as Robbie pushed himself up off the ground and to his knees.

The two brown-haired boys were almost instantly at his side, one reaching a hand down to help him up and the other slapping him on the back as he climbed to his feet. "Man, you almost had him!"

"Good try, Robbie!"

The older of the two boys pointed to where Cowboy had cornered himself against the back fence. "You two go that way," he instructed. "And I'll circle around and get him on the other side."

As the boys raced toward the dog, the plan might have worked if Cowboy hadn't made another escape, this time streaking right between the oldest boy's legs. The sudden move had all three boys collapsing on the ground in laughter.

"Uncle Ryder! Uncle Ryder! Catch Cowboy for us!"

Lindsay didn't know what startled her more, the sudden piercing whistle Ryder gave or that the little boy had called him uncle. She shouldn't have been surprised. Ryder had told her that his brother had two sons and another child on the way. But when Cowboy trotted over to sit at Ryder's feet and obediently dropped the Frisbee as if he hadn't spent the past ten minutes playing keep-away with the toy, and as the boys rushed over, the biggest smile on Robbie's face that Lindsay had seen in a long, long time, she had to face the realization that these weren't just Ryder's nephews...

They were Robbie's cousins.

"Attention, everyone! If I could have your attention." Ryder's brother, Bryce, rose from his spot at the end of the picnic table. The sounds of laughter and conversation continued on around him, but seated beside Ryder, Lindsay saw his hand tighten around the fork he was holding.

When Nina announced that the food was ready and the two dozen or so people had rushed the tables, sitting at Ryder's side hadn't been part of Lindsay's plan. But after loading down their plates to nearly overflowing, the boys, including Robbie, had taken spots at the smallest of the three tables. Her appetite gone, Lindsay had ignored heaping bowls of macaroni salad and potato salad, platters piled high with burgers surrounded by all the fixings, desserts ranging from cookies to brownies to apple pie. Her plate looked bare in comparison, topped with nothing more than a naked hot dog and small handful of chips.

Near the end of the food line, by the time Lindsay grabbed a soda from the ice-filled cooler most of the spots at the tables were taken. The lone empty spot was the place Ryder had saved for her. When she first took her seat, she would rather have crawled beneath the table than sit at Ryder's side, but now...

His knuckles had whitened, the tendons in the back of his hand flexed and Lindsay half expected the plastic utensil to snap in half. The rest of the table went on eating, but Ryder—and Lindsay—knew what was coming.

When his voice failed to claim anyone's attention, Bryce let out a shrill whistle—apparently a Kincaid trait—that had people cringing and complaining before they finally fell silent. "Thank you all for coming over today. It's always great to have our family and friends together."

His broad grin took in his wife and kids before moving on to his parents and Ryder. Nina had filled Lindsay in earlier with the news that Bryce and Ryder's sister, Sydney, who lived in Seattle, couldn't make it to the barbecue but that she would be visiting in a few weeks. "I'll let everyone get back to their food in a minute, but first I have an announcement to make." As Nina cleared her throat, Bryce amended, "We have an announcement to make."

"Oh." The soft exclamation broke from Julia Kincaid's lips a split second before she covered her mouth with her fingertips. Her husband, Ryan, an older, stockier version of his two sons, shot her a quizzical glance, but Bryce didn't leave his father wondering for long.

"Nina and I are having another baby!"

Cheers rang out around the tables, led by the elder Kincaids. Julia immediately jumped up from her seat to hug her son and daughter-in-law while both Bryce and Ryan grinned like the proud papas they were.

"Oh, I do hope it's a girl this time!" Julia exclaimed.

"Hey." Bryce raised his hands in protest. "What's wrong with boys?"

"Absolutely nothing," his mother assured them. "But I already have two grandsons."

Three grandsons. You have three *grandsons.*

Lindsay's hands dropped to her lap, where she kept a

stranglehold on a napkin as if her grip on the flimsy paper was all that was keeping her emotions under control.

She wanted to run, to hide, to bury herself in one of the holes Cowboy had gotten in trouble for digging earlier. She wanted—

At her side, Ryder cleared his throat. He reached for the glass in front of him, gulped down half the contents, his throat working as he swallowed. He was the only Kincaid still seated, the only one who hadn't crowded around Bryce and Nina, and it wouldn't be long before one of them noticed.

A muscle jumped in Ryder's jaw, a sign of the emotions struggling inside him. Lindsay's grip on the napkin loosened, and she let go of her own battle with her conscience. Had her actions ten years ago been those of a selfless mother, concerned only for her child? Or had they been the selfish decision of a heartbroken girl who was only thinking of herself?

She didn't know.

There were hundreds of things she could have done differently in the past decade, but only one thing she wanted to do right then.

Reaching over, she wrapped her fingers around the hand Ryder had pressed against his thigh. At first he didn't move, but gradually the rock-hard tension eased as he unclenched his fist and turned his wrist to intertwine his fingers with hers. Such a simple thing. Holding hands. Something small children did on playgrounds and during field trips. It could have been—should have been— completely innocent.

And yet the subtle press of palms, the heat of his skin warming hers, the yielding of her narrow fingers to the width of Ryder's, none of it felt innocent or simple... Least of all the desire pooling low in her belly.

His shoulders rose on a deep breath, and she gave his

hand a final squeeze before he pushed away from the table. He gave his brother a back-thumping hug and kissed his sister-in-law on the cheek. "I said it before, but congratulations, both of you. My new niece or nephew is lucky enough to have the greatest parents." He shot a smile to his own mother and father. "After you guys, of course."

"Oh, of course!" His mother laughed.

Ryder slipped back to his seat as the rest of their friends wanted their turns at congratulating the couple. Sincerity shone in his green eyes as he glanced over at Lindsay. "Thank you."

"You don't have to thank me." *Please don't thank me. Don't...be nice to me. And stop* looking *at me like that!*

"I meant what I said earlier, Lindsay. I'd like a chance for us to start over."

"As friends?"

The corner of his mouth kicked up in a wry smile. "We were more than friends."

For one night, they'd been lovers. One night that had changed both of their lives more than Ryder could possibly know.

Lindsay swallowed. "Ryder, I...I can't. We can't go back. It's not possible."

"And what about going forward? Is that impossible, too?" Reading the answer in her gaze, he came to his own conclusion as he eased away from her on the crowded bench. "Because you can't forgive me for what happened."

"It's not that," Lindsay protested quietly. "It's—"

That when I tell you the truth about what really happened that night, I don't know how you'll ever be able to forgive me.

Chapter Nine

How long had it been, Ryder wondered, since he'd waited outside a girl's house hoping to catch a glimpse of her?

Not during his relationship with Brittany, that was for sure. From the moment she moved to Clearville after her parents' divorce, she'd made her interest in Ryder well-known. An interest he'd wholeheartedly returned, bowled over by the beauty and sophistication of the girl from San Francisco.

So that had to make it...eighth grade? Back when he had a crush on Tori Woods, who'd lived a block over from where he'd grown up.

Assuming that he had grown up, he thought wryly as he shifted on the truck's leather seat and kept his eye on Ellie's Victorian. He could have simply climbed the new steps leading up to the porch and knocked on the door Lindsay had finished painting before the barbecue. Ellie would have welcomed him even though it was Saturday morning and he wasn't scheduled to work. She'd offer him another mouthwatering breakfast that would make the slightly burned toast and eggs he'd scrambled earlier taste like cafeteria leftovers in comparison. As he sat at their table, Robbie would likely rehash the previous evening's fun. Playing with Ryder's nephews and trying to catch the ever-elusive Cowboy as he had done on the ride home.

And Lindsay would nod to prove she was listening. She'd smile and thank him again for a great evening, but not once would she meet his gaze. Just as she'd avoided looking him in the eye when she said goodbye on the front porch last night before racing inside as if she were the one past her bedtime rather than Robbie.

Oh, she'd said all the right things—it had been a long day, Robbie was tired from all the running around he'd done and she needed to get him upstairs to take a bath and brush his teeth before hitting the sack. And Ryder didn't question her dedication to her son, but that didn't make him any less certain that her words were little more than an excuse to avoid having a conversation with him without her grandmother and son around.

Which was why Ryder hadn't climbed the front porch steps to knock on the door and why he was still sitting in his vehicle outside her house like an eighth grader with a crush. Or like a psycho stalker. Take your pick.

"This is all your fault, Bryce," Ryder muttered beneath his breath. Not only had his brother been the one to suggest inviting Lindsay to the barbecue in the first place, but his brother and sister-in-law had also been the ones to corner him at the end of the night when Ellie and Lindsay both insisted on staying late to help clean up despite the Kincaids' protests.

"I like her," Nina had said with a knowing smile Ryder easily translated into *You like her.*

"We're friends, Nina. Don't make this into something it's not." Especially when he wasn't even sure he could make a friendship out of the scattered pieces he'd left in his wake ten years ago.

Not that either Bryce or Nina knew anything about the one night he'd spent with Lindsay. He'd been so careful for Lindsay's sake—and his own, he'd now admit—that no one knew.

"Lindsay's only here for a few weeks—"

"So?" his brother interrupted. "A few weeks is plenty of time to go out and have a good time."

Ryder shot his brother a glare. "She's not like that, Bryce." Ryder had already left town and moved into the dorms at college by the time news of Lindsay's pregnancy hit the Clearville grapevine, but he could only imagine what that had been like for her.

Bryce rolled his eyes. "So don't have *that* good a time. She's a single mom raising a kid on her own. Take her out for a movie or to dinner. Get your feet wet in the dating pool before diving in again."

"What your brother is trying so metaphorically to say is that going out with Lindsay doesn't have to be serious for either one of you. Like you said, she's only here for a few weeks, so just…have fun." His sister-in-law gave him a quick hug. "We all want you to be happy."

No one in his family knew the whole story behind his divorce, but Ryder supposed it didn't take a genius to figure out his marriage to Brittany hadn't been a happy one especially toward the end. But he and Brittany had been together for so long that he could barely remember what it was like to ask a girl out.

As much as he hated to admit it, Bryce's and Nina's words had given him a boost of encouragement he needed. It helped, too, knowing his family liked Lindsay.

Seeing her talking and laughing with Nina, once he'd convinced himself they weren't necessarily dissecting him on a platter, he'd realized how Lindsay…fit.

Despite overdressing for the occasion, Lindsay had been quick to lend a hand even as she'd kept an eye on Robbie and Ellie. With Lindsay's innate shyness, Ryder knew it wasn't easy for her to make a place for herself in a crowd and yet, with his family, she had done so. Her genuine kindness had shone through her protective shell, and his family had welcomed her—the way they'd never really welcomed Brittany.

"Be careful with that one, son," had been his dad's advice.

"Don't get too serious, too soon, Ry. Brittany isn't the only girl you're ever going to date," his mother had told him.

"She's trouble," Bryce had said, *"with a capital B-I-T—"*

That was as far as his older brother got in his spelling lesson before Ryder punched him in the face. It wasn't the first fight or the last he'd gotten into over Brittany, who'd never been one to shy away from the drama.

Ryder turned his head to the side, working out the kinks and tension just thinking of his ex could cause. Life would have been very different if he'd listened to his family back then. Maybe things would start to look up if he listened to them now.

But when Ellie's front door opened, the jump in Ryder's pulse had nothing to do with his family's approval and everything to do with the woman who stepped outside. He had to smile a little at the studious look on Lindsay's face as she gazed at her phone. If he didn't know better, he would have thought she was on her way to a business meeting.

Her hair was caught back at the nape of her neck with a ribbon. A black skirt swirled around her knees, topped by a sleeveless cream-colored silky blouse with a coordinating pinstripe. Shiny patent leather pumps with a small bow on the toes and a matching bag completed an outfit far too stylish for the day she had planned. He'd overheard her tell Nina that she was hitting the stores today, shopping for finishes for the kitchen remodeling—next on his list once the porch was completed.

Ellie had given Lindsay carte blanche on the decision making, and Ryder had already supplied her with the measurements needed for new tile floors and countertops and backsplash. He'd also given her the names of places to shop in nearby Redfield. He'd be willing to bet Lindsay already had those stores' addresses programmed into an app that would map out the fastest route from one store to the next.

She was so focused on her phone as she walked down the driveway that he was almost beside her before she looked up with a startled glance. "Ryder, what are you doing here?"

"I heard you say you were going shopping today and figured I'd offer my expertise."

"Because you're an expert shopper?" Doubt filled her voice, not that he blamed her. The thought of going to the mall was enough to make him break out in hives, but when it came to home improvement and hardware stores, no aisle was left unturned.

"I am when it comes to that list you've got programmed into your phone."

Lindsay's chin lifted as she tucked the phone into her purse. "There's nothing wrong with having a plan, especially when there's still so much work to do. Speaking of which, when will the porch be finished? I was hoping you'd have the interiors started by next week."

"You think that's going to work?" he asked softly.

"Do I—" Lindsay blinked up at him. "Will what work?"

"Do you think treating me like the hired help will make either one of us forget about that kiss?"

It was a risky move to bring up the kiss, but he hadn't missed the slight tremor in her hand as she pulled out her car keys or the small step she took, moving out of his reach as if mere inches could diffuse the attraction building between them.

"It was a mistake, so yes, I do want to forget about it."

"And if I disagree?"

"That doesn't matter since it can't happen again."

"Can't, Lindsay?" She was too much of a stickler when it came to grammar for him not to catch her choice of words. "Because I really think it could. I mean, anything that happens once can always happen again."

Her fingers fumbled for the fob on the key chain, but instead of unlocking the car, she hit the wrong button. She jumped as the alarm blared, and the keys clattered against the driveway.

Ryder bent down to scoop them up and calmly deactivated the alarm. "You were saying?"

"That it *won't* happen again."

Giving an agreeable nod, Ryder said, "Okay," before pocketing her key chain in the front pocket of his jeans and taking a few steps back toward the street.

"Ryder—what are you doing? Give me back my keys!"

"Thought we'd take my truck instead. It makes more sense considering all the stuff you need to buy. I'll be able to haul most of it in the back, and then you won't have to pay delivery fees."

He could see he'd stumped her with the sound logic of his argument and carefully hid his grin.

"That does make sense," she admitted, dragging the words out slowly as if wanting to give herself opportunity to call them back. "But I'm going to pay you for your time."

"Back to the hired help, are we?" Before she had a chance to argue, he said, "Fine. You can buy me lunch, and we'll be even."

Lindsay's jaw dropped as she followed Ryder inside the enormous warehouse. The cavernous space was filled with row after row of stone, tile and wood—some stacked in boxes, others on pallets and lining metal shelves. Sensing that she was lagging behind, Ryder glanced over his shoulder with a kid-in-a-candy-store grin. "Come on! Let's get started."

"Started?" She didn't have a clue where to even begin. "Ryder, wait! I thought—" Lowering her voice, she said, "I was expecting some kind of, I don't know, sales center where a designer would help with all this…stuff."

"Designers work on commission, so the more they get you to spend, the more money they make. Wholesale places like this don't have commissions and eliminate a lot of the overhead. You'll get a great deal, and they still have plenty of products to choose from."

"Lack of selection isn't the issue. This place is huge, and I don't even know what I'm looking for." Feeling a sense of near desperation, Lindsay grabbed for the phone she'd tucked away in her purse. She'd started a Pinterest page pinned with photos of kitchens she and Ellie both liked. Maybe if she had a visual reference—

Ryder's hand closed over hers and the phone she clung to like a lifeline. "Relax, Lindsay. This'll be fun." He waved a hand. "Imagine it's all a bunch of shoes."

"Seriously, Ryder. Shoes?"

"Are you telling me you don't like shoes?" His pointed gaze dropped to the black kitten heels she wore.

"Yes, okay, I like shoes. But I don't see what that has to do with any of this."

"It's all about finding what you like. You like sexy shoes that match your outfits."

Heat flooded Lindsay's cheeks. "They're not sexy."

"Oh, yes, they are. On you, they are."

Her blush only increased at the look in his eyes, but when she thought he'd push for more, Ryder took a step back. "Picking out tile is simply about finding a look you like that coordinates with the rest of the kitchen."

From there, he went on to explain the differences between ceramic and porcelain and natural stone. About decorative listelles for accents and metal dots that could be inserted into the cut corners of the tile. He suggested a mosaic tile for the backsplash, showing her shiny sheets of colorful glass, so smooth she couldn't resist running her fingers over the surface.

"They sell granite slabs for countertops here, too. Of course, they'd have to come out and template once the cabinets are in, but they'll be able to give an accurate estimate based on the square footage and basic layout." Reaching out, he pulled her closer to his side, out of the way of a forklift rolling by—overhead strobe light flashing and backup alarm beeping. "So, what do you think?"

Expectation filled his expression, and for once Lindsay would rather blame her mind going blank on the warm grip of his hand against her arm than admit she was totally overwhelmed. Casting about almost blindly, she let her gaze land on a tile a few feet away. "That one's…nice. It's a porcelain, right? And a good, neutral color."

Ryder didn't have to say a word for her to know he wasn't impressed. "What?" she demanded, feeling as if she'd failed some kind of test. "You're the one who said it was a good substitute for natural stone since it's less expensive and easier to maintain."

"Hey, all that's true, but are you really sure you want to go with 'neutral'?"

"This isn't about me," she argued, ignoring the voice in her head that reminded her how her condo was decorated mostly in shades of beige. "This is about picking out products that will be appealing to potential buyers once the house goes up for sale."

Ryder offered a noncommittal sound in response, and

Lindsay couldn't blame him. It wasn't as if she'd been making great headway in convincing Ellie to sell.

"Okay, so you're the expert. Which one do you like?"

"I know you and Ellie are thinking of sticking with white cabinets." Ryder had told her he would have gladly refurbished the cabinets had they been original to the house, but the cupboards had been replaced throughout the decades, most recently sometime in the eighties, which accounted for the dated, whitewash finish. "But there's no reason why you can't pick a contrasting tile. Some people shy away from warmer tones, afraid the space will seem too dark, but I think it makes a small room cozier. Intimate, even."

Cozy. Intimate. The words didn't bring images of a kitchen to mind. Instead thoughts of naked limbs entwined in front of a golden, roaring fire teased her senses...

Too bad Ryder didn't work on commission, Lindsay thought. With his husky voice and the tempting heat in his gaze, any red-blooded woman would be willing to buy whatever he was selling.

"Will everything be okay in your truck?" Lindsay asked, looking back at her hard-won purchases sitting exposed in the truck bed. After going back and forth with an embarrassing amount of indecision, she'd finally decided on a slate-look tile in a mix of blues, grays and gold along with black granite countertops and a metal backsplash that was reminiscent of vintage tin ceiling panels.

Ryder didn't break stride as he guided her toward the restaurant with his hand staking a familiar and possessive claim at the small of her back. "Come on, city girl. It took a forklift to load all that stuff, remember? It's not going anywhere, and you owe me lunch."

"I owe you more than lunch," she admitted as his hand slipped away when he reached for the swinging door to the barbecue joint they'd chosen. His dark eyebrows rose suggestively, prompting Lindsay to wryly add, "Not that much more."

His low chuckle followed her as she stepped into the family-style restaurant with dark-paneled walls and a Western theme. She waited until the hostess seated them at a small table topped with a red-and-white-gingham-checked tablecloth and the waitress came by to take their drink orders to say, "Thank you for not making me feel like even more of an idiot."

Ryder frowned. "Why would you feel like an idiot in the first place?"

Lindsay shrugged as she squeezed a wedge of lemon into her water. "For not being able to make up my mind over something as simple as picking out tile."

"It's not simple," he argued. "That's why interior designers make a decent living helping people with those decisions. Besides, the way I figure it, I owed *you*. How many free periods did you give up our senior year to tutor me in calculus? And not once did you make me feel like a dumb jock."

"You were never a dumb jock," Lindsay argued, choosing to focus on the second part of Ryder's comments and not on the first. No reason for him to know she would have done anything he asked back then, especially if it meant getting to spend more time with him.

"Thanks, I knew it was important to keep my grades up if I wanted to qualify for a scholarship. Just like I wanted college to be about more than football and frat parties." A wicked grin broke free as he admitted, "Not that football and partying didn't play a big role during those four years. But I knew I was going to have to find a career after college, and that it wouldn't be playing in the pros."

His words were matter-of-fact, and Lindsay almost reluctantly said, "I remember when you were offered that athletic scholarship. Everyone thought it was the first step to seeing you play on a national stage."

"Yeah, me, too. But…" His gaze dropped to the straw wrapper he'd been folding into shapes before looking back up to meet her gaze. "I wasn't that good."

"You were amazing!" Lindsay exclaimed like the cheerleader she'd never been.

His smile was wry as he pointed out, "I was great here in Clearville, where the competition was limited. But in college…the guys riding the bench for the defense were the same size as the starters in the NFL, and I was this scrawny eighteen-year-old kid from the boondocks. I pretty much spent all four years holding a clipboard on the sidelines."

"I'm sorry, Ryder."

"Sometimes, so am I. But then most of the time, I figure it was the best worst thing that could have happened to me. Here, I was the hometown hero who could do no wrong. I thought I was invincible. That life would be as easy as it was in high school, and everything would always go my way. I needed that smackdown. I deserved it. For the way I treated you, if for no other reason."

"Ryder…"

"I have changed, Lindsay. I hope you can see I'm not that same guy. I know this will probably sound crazy, but I…I've missed you. I've missed our friendship, and I don't think I realized how much until you came back. And if you don't believe that and if you can't forgive me, well, I can't blame you. But I meant what I said when I asked for a second chance."

The sincerity in his gaze pulled Lindsay in, and she felt herself tumbling deeper as he held out his upturned palm. Not touching her but waiting for her to make the move of meeting him halfway.

Maybe Ryder had changed, but something of the teenage girl Lindsay had once been must have still lived inside, because she found herself reaching for his hand. Agreeing to anything he asked as long as it meant getting to spend more time with him.

"I think we could both use a second chance."

Chapter Ten

They might have agreed to put the past behind them, but for Ryder, simply sitting across the table from Lindsay and holding her hand made him feel like an eager kid again. Her fingers felt delicate and soft against his calloused, work-roughened palm, and the simple touch had his blood heating in his veins.

The sights and sounds of the restaurant around them—waitresses weaving in and out of tables, platters loaded with smoky barbecued chicken and ribs, the clink of silverware and the hum of conversation—faded away. Losing himself in the hopeful glow of Lindsay's blue-green gaze and the pounding of his own pulse, he was tempted to close the space between them and claim her slightly parted lips with his own. The mirrored longing reflected in her expression only added to his own desire.

Slow, he reminded himself. *You're taking things slow this time.*

And doing it right. Lindsay might have forgiven him,

but he wasn't sure he'd forgiven himself. He wanted to romance Lindsay, to treat her the way she deserved. He wanted the wariness shadowing her fine features to disappear, the hesitation still shaking her to solidify into the certainty that she could trust him. And he couldn't rush that.

But it was still with a great deal of reluctance that he let go when the buzz of a phone sounded. "Sorry," she said as she slid her hand from his and reached into her bag. "I need to make sure it's not Ellie or Robbie." She frowned as she swiped her finger across the screen and read the message.

"Everything okay?" he asked.

"It's fine. A friend of mine from work sent me an update on a memo that went out the other day." Sighing, she said, "I was afraid something like this would happen. I'd hoped it wouldn't, but…"

"Something like what?"

"The company I work for was recently bought out by one of its competitors. The new owners came in and said there'd be a place for all of us and nothing would change." She gave a soft laugh. "Of course, we are talking about another PR company. Naturally they'd put the best spin on the buyout, wouldn't they?"

"Is your job—"

"Safe for the moment. But they're having everyone reapply for positions most of us have held for years, and they've let go of some of the part-time employees, consolidating some of the positions and dividing the workload between the rest of the team."

"From what I hear from Ellie, you're good at your job, Lindsay. They'd be foolish to let you go."

She blushed a little at his praise. "According to my friend's email, the new boss is looking for 'go-getters' and is waiting for us to 'wow' him. I've spent the past six years wowing my old boss to get where I am. I've worked nights and weekends, putting in the long hours because

I told myself I was securing my future. Robbie's future. And now I feel like all that hard work's been erased and I'm starting from scratch." With a shake of her head, she tucked her phone back in her purse and said, "Sorry, you don't need to hear me complain."

"You're not complaining, and I don't mind. You were always willing to listen to me."

She leaned forward as she swirled her straw through the ice in her glass. "You were just trying to distract me from the homework we were supposed to be doing."

"No," he protested with mock seriousness. "Okay, maybe I was. But I also know you were a great listener, and I always felt I could trust you. So maybe this is my chance to return the favor. You said you hoped this wouldn't happen, but obviously you thought it might. Knowing you, that means you must have a backup plan already in place."

"Not a plan, exactly, although I have updated my résumé and even talked to one of those companies that headhunts for corporations. But a new job would mean working my way up again, too, which wouldn't be any different than staying where I am." She gave a small laugh. "You know, when they told me I had to take all my vacation time or I would lose it, I thought I'd go crazy not working for six weeks. Even after I'd made plans to come here, knowing all the work that needed to be done at Gran's house, I felt like I would be facing this huge void. No conference calls, no meetings, no constant emails... How would I survive?"

"I thought the same thing moving back here. I couldn't wait to leave after graduation. If you told me I'd be back in ten years, I would have said you were crazy. That there's nothing for me here."

"And now?"

"Now I've had one of those moments every child dreads. The moment when he realizes his parents were right all along. Clearville's...home. It's everything I hated as a kid—small town, slow paced, low profile. It hasn't changed."

"But you have," she said softly.

Ryder's pulse pounded a low, simmering beat at the quiet certainty in her voice, and their gazes locked for a lingering moment. He had to clear his throat before saying, "Yeah, I have."

"You know, I, um, think Ellie's been cooking some kind of plan behind my back to try to get me to stay in town."

"Really? Huh, behind your back and everything. Kinda like fixing her house with the idea of putting it on the market…"

"Are you saying I'm like my grandmother?"

"I might be. After all, Ellie's an amazing woman."

A touch of pink rose in Lindsay's cheeks. "That she is. A sneaky one, too."

"So, how's she trying to get you to stay in town?"

"Somehow she found out that the Chamber of Commerce has an open position in PR and marketing. Someone to come in and get the word out about Clearville. To increase tourism and maybe bring in new businesses, as well."

"Sounds like it could be right up your alley."

"I don't know…"

"Not ready to give up the limelight and those television spots?"

"Hardly."

"Then maybe it's not such a bad idea to see what the job has to offer. You know Clearville's a great place to grow up, to raise a family…"

"Maybe you should be the one working for the Chamber of Commerce," Lindsay said wryly.

"Maybe," Ryder agreed, keeping his voice light despite the realization shaking him. It wasn't half a dozen new businesses he'd like to see move to Clearville.

Just one single mom and her son.

* * *

It wouldn't hurt to go inside and look around, Lindsay told herself as she stood outside the Chamber of Commerce building on Monday morning. She was simply going inside to talk to Patricia Bennett, to see what help and advice she might be able to give.

Nothing more than that.

But between the texts she'd exchanged with some of her work friends over the weekend, and the look of contentment and belonging in Ryder's expression as he'd said, "Clearville's…home," simply standing outside the small building felt as though she'd already taken a big step.

One that would keep her in town permanently?

"It's a conversation, not a commitment," she mumbled beneath her breath as she reached for the handle on the front door. The Chamber of Commerce shared space with the local tourism center in a charming, narrow Victorian that had been renovated into business suites. Lindsay followed a sign down a short hall to their offices.

"Lindsay! Hi, I'm so glad you could stop by." Patricia smiled and circled around the long counter dividing the reception area from the back office. "And just in time, too." The woman waved at a series of photographs spread out over the space. "I've been working with one of the local businesses—a ranch called the Rockin' R—to put together some flyers and brochures. Have you heard of it?"

When Lindsay shook her head, Patricia explained, "It's a riding stable outside town. They offer lessons and trail rides and have expanded to include half a dozen or so rental cabins. The owner, Jarrett Deeks, used to ride in the rodeo, and he also runs an equine rescue out of the ranch."

Lindsay glanced through the photos. Many were landscapes taken around the property—images of towering trees rising to a cloudless cobalt sky, gently rolling hills covered in lush summer grasses and wildflowers, a crystal-clear stream cutting through a meadow. The others were of horses. The photographer had done an excellent job capturing each one's personality—a sweet-faced chestnut peering out from a stall, a small gray mare in a corral, her face turned slightly away as if camera-shy, and a proud black beast who seemed to gaze right out of the picture as if making a challenge.

"These are wonderful."

"Jarrett's sister took them. For the past month or so, Jarrett and his fiancée have been working on a fund-raiser to bring attention to the rescue. With his connections, they've decided on a benefit rodeo."

"That's a great idea."

"We think so, too. We've been working with them to come up with ways to promote the event…and the town. I'd love to get your opinion on how to get the word out. When Jarrett first came up with the idea, he wanted to rush right in, but Theresa helped convince him that it would be better to wait until summer and tourist season. With kids being out of school, we'll draw more families, and with any luck, the weather will be perfect."

"Theresa?" Lindsay echoed.

"Yes, Jarrett's fiancée." The bell over the door rang, and Patricia glanced over Lindsay's shoulder with a smile. "And here she is now! Lindsay, have you met Theresa Pirelli?"

Shock made Lindsay feel as if she were moving in slow motion as she turned around. She hadn't seen Tony's sister in ten years, but she would have recognized the brunette who stepped through the doorway in an instant. Theresa still had the same shoulder-length dark hair, the same piercing blue eyes, the same classic features that had matured her from a pretty girl into a beautiful woman.

"Lindsay works at a PR firm in Phoenix," Patricia was saying, "and she's willing to take a look at our marketing platform to see what else we might do to promote the rodeo."

The other woman looked at her eagerly, waiting for lightbulb moments to start flashing around like cameras at a kindergarten play, while Theresa simply watched. Lindsay couldn't begin to read her expression. Couldn't imagine what she was thinking...

"Radio spots," Lindsay blurted out. She didn't know if it was a lightbulb going off, but she'd at least managed to hit a switch and turn on business mode. "Not promotional airtime, because that would be too expensive, but if you were invited to call in as a guest on one of the morning shows, that would be some great publicity. Patricia said your fiancé used to be in the rodeo, so a country-western station would be a perfect fit.

"And have you thought of doing any raffles? The prizes could be riding lessons at the stables or a stay at the cabins. Maybe some of the other local businesses would want to get involved and donate as well, since they, too, will benefit from the crowds the rodeo draws."

For the next hour, Lindsay and the other two women tossed around more suggestions for expanding the ranch's social media outlets, updating the website to include a PayPal link for donations and opportunities for people to sponsor the horses up for adoption as well as creating personality profiles for the animals—similar to what could be found on an internet dating site.

"That would be one site where a girl could go looking for a stud, and she'd have a good chance of actually finding one," Theresa said wryly after Lindsay proposed that idea.

She'd half expected Theresa to veto all her plans on principle alone, but she'd listened instead, agreeing with many of the suggestions and offering to talk with Jarrett about others.

But when Patricia stepped away to speak with a coworker, leaving Lindsay and Theresa on their own, the ideas and conversation came to such an abrupt halt that Lindsay's ears rang with the dull buzz of silence that stretched on and on...

Unable to take it any longer, she asked, "How's Tony?"

Theresa blinked, taken aback by Lindsay calling out the elephant in the middle of the room. "Fine. We don't see him as often as we'd like."

The words were as smooth and calm as a crystal lake, making Lindsay wonder if she'd imagined the currents raging beneath.

The Pirelli family had come down hard on Tony—telling him to man up, to take responsibility, to do the right thing. Long before word of her pregnancy fired through the local grapevine, Tony had been the black sheep in his otherwise perfect family, but the rift in his relationship was yet another burden she carried.

"Let 'em think the worst about me," he'd said, his bad-boy sneer on full display. *"They always do."*

And they had. When Lindsay refused to talk about the father of her baby and Tony deflected the accusations with protests designed to make him look even more responsible— *"Hey, maybe the kid's not even mine"*—people had made up their own minds.

"The two of you didn't—" Theresa hesitated, and this time Lindsay definitely picked up on a ripple or two. "—stay in touch?"

"The first few years, when he was in the marines, we exchanged letters and emails." She'd sent him some pictures of Robbie as a baby and later as a toddler. She wasn't sure which of them stopped writing first.

In Clearville, they'd had something in common. They'd both been loners, both a little lonely, both on the outside looking in. They'd been teenagers. But after that last summer, they'd grown up fast. Lindsay had found her foot-

ing in college and in motherhood. Even in his letters, she
had sensed how Tony had matured from a sullen boy to a
hardened solider.

She didn't think they'd have much in common anymore.

Still, she'd been relieved when he wrote to tell her he
was getting out of the marines especially after another
friend of hers in the service, a boy she'd met in college,
had been killed overseas.

"Where is he living now?"

"All over. He works in private security—traveling with
high-powered executives, shadowing the hottest celebri-
ties. I thought I caught a glimpse of him in the background
during one of those red-carpet interviews."

"A bodyguard…" Lindsay shook her head, a feeling of
nostalgia tugging at her heartstrings like the melody of an
almost-forgotten song. "Somehow that fits."

And maybe a small part of the boy she'd once known
still remained.

After all, he'd sacrificed a great deal to protect her.

Theresa sighed. "Yes, I've always thought so, too."

For a brief moment, Lindsay grasped on to the hope
that this meeting—one that could have been so awkward,
so filled with the potential of tearing open old wounds—
might actually end on a positive note… And then her cell
phone rang.

She'd pulled it out of her purse earlier to view the
Rockin' R website and had left it sitting on the counter.
Harmlessly sitting there, she'd thought, until the screen
flashed to life with Robbie's smiling face shining out in
full HD color.

Theresa froze as she stared at the picture, her blue eyes
turning so cold Lindsay could almost see ice crystals form-
ing in the irises. "Whatever happened between you and
Tony is your business. But robbing my parents of the op-

portunity to get to know their grandchild…that was pure selfishness on your part, Lindsay."

"Lindsay, is everything all right?"

She glanced up as Ellie stepped into the spare bedroom later that evening. She'd driven around for most of the afternoon after leaving the Chamber of Commerce. She hadn't wanted to come straight home, but she certainly hadn't wanted to stay in town. She'd taken the back roads, driving aimlessly in circles, finally slamming on the brakes when she reached an arched wooden sign over a long gravel driveway.

The Rockin' R Ranch.

If she'd still clung to any hope that she might be able to put the past behind her, that sign was yet another reminder that she couldn't escape.

"I stopped by to see Patricia at the Chamber of Commerce this morning."

Ellie's eyes lit in excitement. "That's wonderful! How did it go?"

"It was…horrible." Lindsay glanced down at the shirt in her hands, at the stack of laundry, piled high in the rocking chair. She kept folding and refolding that same shirt as she thought about throwing her clothes into a suitcase instead of a drawer and driving back to Phoenix as fast as possible.

"What happened? Patricia Bennett should be thrilled to have you on board—"

"It wasn't Patricia." Before Lindsay left, the other woman had made it clear the job was hers—should she decide to stay in town. Something she wouldn't—she couldn't—do. "She wasn't the problem. It was…Theresa Pirelli."

Ellie's eyes widened behind her wire-framed glasses. "Oh."

After filling her grandmother in on what had happened, Lindsay finally let the wrinkled-beyond-recognition blouse fall from her hands. "I just stood there. I didn't know what to say, what explanation I could possibly give to justify what I'd done…"

"Well," Ellie said after a prolonged silence, "I suppose you could have told the truth—that Tony *isn't* Robbie's father."

Shock stole the air from Lindsay's lungs. She gaped at her grandmother, too stunned to do anything else, as Ellie took her by the hand and led her to sit on the foot of the bed. "You…you knew? All this time…"

Ellie shook her gray head. "No, I thought Tony was Robbie's father even though you refused to talk about it back then. You were good friends, and, well, that was how my relationship with your grandfather started."

Friends who fell in love, married and enjoyed a long successful marriage filled with children, grandchildren and great-grandchildren, love, laughter and even some tears.

"So I know how friendship can turn into something more. You and Tony were almost inseparable that last summer before he joined the marines, and of course by the time you told your parents you were pregnant, Ryder had already left for college, so no one considered that he might be the one."

And the hits just keep coming. Lindsay dropped her face into her hands. "How did you figure out that Ryder…?"

"Little things at first. Seeing Ryder and Robbie together. Watching Robbie with Ryder's nephews. The pictures hanging in Bryce's house from when he and Ryder were boys. Putting all those pieces together was enough to make me wonder, and then there was you."

"Me?" she echoed, looking up into her grandmother's knowing expression.

Ellie smiled gently. "You never looked at Tony the way you look at Ryder."

Swallowing hard, Lindsay didn't ask, too afraid of what else her grandmother might have noticed. "When I heard he and Brittany had divorced and that he'd moved back to Clearville, I came back to tell him."

"But you haven't."

Unable to sit still, she bounced off the mattress. The queen-size bed took up most of the spare bedroom. The journey from the closet on one side to the chair tucked into the other corner took no more than five steps, not nearly enough room to outdistance the guilt hounding her. "I need a little more time."

"It's been ten years, Lindsay."

"No," she argued adamantly. "It's only been six months. Six months since Ryder's divorce. Before that—" Before that, Ryder had been with Brittany. He'd always been with Brittany, and Lindsay hadn't had any intention of telling Ryder he had a son as long as the two of them were together. Sharing Robbie with his father was one thing. Sharing him with an evil stepmother—no, that wasn't going to happen.

"And I've been back for less than two weeks." She'd needed that time to get to know him, to learn about the real Ryder Kincaid and not the golden boy she'd had a crush on in high school. "I still have plenty of time left to tell Ryder about Robbie before we go back home."

Ellie heaved a disappointed sigh. "Don't you think it's time for you to rethink your plans to go back to Phoenix?"

"Rethink…" Meeting her grandmother's gaze, Lindsay was surprised by the steely expression written in her softly lined face. "You mean stay here? Gran, I have a job. I have a whole life back in Phoenix."

Well, she had a job at least. For now. Assuming her position wasn't being sliced apart, divvied into manageable pieces and passed around like a batch of brownies in the lunchroom. First-come, first-served, and Lindsay would be left holding nothing but an empty pan.

"Besides, what about Robbie? He has school and friends there…"

"And he has family *here*. Not Tony's family, but Ryder's. Grandparents, aunts, uncles and cousins who Robbie already refers to as his new best friends. He doesn't have that in Phoenix."

"He has my mom and dad," Lindsay argued, a last-ditch effort, and she knew it.

"Your parents will be retiring in a few years. I don't see any reason why they couldn't come back here."

Lindsay stared at her sweet-faced grandmother. "This is what you've been counting on all long, isn't it?"

Ellie simply smiled. "I do love when a plan comes together."

Chapter Eleven

"Final piece." Kneeling on the wooden floors outside the kitchen, Ryder held up a triangular section of tile. He glanced back at Robbie, and the satisfaction and pride shining behind the boy's round glasses reached out and kickstarted something in his heart. "Wanna do the honors?"

"Yeah!"

Ryder understood the boy's excitement. It was how he felt at the end of every job. Not that the remodeling of Ellie's Victorian was complete. The kitchen with its gleaming white cabinets, granite countertop and new tile floor was a major accomplishment, but Ryder still had other projects to tackle. The laundry room, the bathrooms, the hardwood floors. The list went on, and for once, Ryder wasn't in any hurry to see it end. Not when going to work meant seeing Lindsay every day.

"Like this?" Robbie asked as he carefully set the final piece of tile in the empty space filled with thin-set and

placed the plastic spacers exactly as Ryder had shown him
to do to form the perfect grout line.

"Yep, like that."

Not when coming to work meant having his own helper.
As his mother had been in high school, Robbie was the
perfect student—a fast learner and eager to please.

And when the boy looked up at Ryder in awe after he'd
shown him—from a safe and supervised distance—how
to work the wet saw or how to snap a plumb line or how to
find the studs hidden in the walls, and declared, "Wow, you
know how to do, like, everything," the pride Ryder had felt
in a job well done was nothing compared to the pride he
felt in making even the slightest difference in Robbie's life.

No longer did Robbie talk to his T-shirt, his chin lowered against his chest, when Ryder asked him a question. He held his head a little higher, his shoulders a little
straighter, and Ryder hadn't seen any sign of the computer
games that had once been glued to the boy's hand. Ryder
knew his two nephews shared in the credit. Their joint efforts to capture Cowboy had cemented the boys' friendship, and Bryce and Nina had invited Robbie over to play
more than once in the past two weeks.

Robbie was a happier boy, and when Ryder would find
Lindsay watching them, her blue-green gaze softened with
love and caring, Ryder felt, well, another kick start, though
not necessarily to his heart.

Taking things slow was hell on his self-control, especially with Lindsay on hand for the remodeling. She'd
helped with demoing the old countertops and dismantling
the cabinets. Her enthusiasm in swinging a sledgehammer
had been as sexy as hell. A little scary, too.

Working side by side in the cramped kitchen—sometimes
laughing, sometimes arguing, always aware of the sexual
tension simmering below the surface—Ryder didn't know

how many times he'd been tempted to reach out, grab Lindsay and pull her into his arms.

But then he'd remember how she ran from their last kiss and knew he had to be patient. So he contented himself—or maybe tortured himself was a better description—with the occasional touch on her arm, the casual brush of his hand against the small of her back, a joking waltz around the tiny kitchen when they'd bumped into each other's personal space for the fourth or fifth time.

The frustration would have been enough to make Ryder pull his hair out if he hadn't heard Lindsay's breath catch even at those innocent touches, if he hadn't felt an answering spark, if he hadn't seen the growing heat and awareness in the sidelong looks when she thought he wasn't watching.

He'd messed up big-time before, and he wasn't about to blow this second chance. She hadn't said much about the meeting she'd had over at the Chamber of Commerce. As far as he knew, the position was still open. He couldn't imagine Patricia Bennett not offering Lindsay the job if she'd been interested, which meant Lindsay's plans hadn't changed.

Maybe he was a fool to start something that would end with Lindsay leaving to go back to Phoenix in less than a month. Getting close only to have to let go. Or maybe the built-in expiration date made the whole idea of dating again easier, safer somehow. As Nina had said, neither he nor Lindsay had to worry about taking the relationship too seriously.

Ryder swallowed a snort. Not that he and Lindsay had a relationship or had even gone out on a date for that matter.

"It looks awesome, Ryder! Wait till I tell Tyler and Brayden I helped." Robbie interrupted his thoughts as he jumped to his feet with the last piece of tile firmly in place.

"Helped? Tell those nephews of mine I couldn't have done it without you, bud."

"All right!"

Robbie reached over to give what started out as a high five, but the boy's eager momentum had him bumping up against Ryder's side. Pure instinct had Ryder's arm going around the boy's shoulders to steady him, and before he knew it, Robbie had wrapped his arms around him in a quick hug.

"Thanks, Ryder," he whispered.

Caught off guard by the lump in his throat, Ryder coughed a bit before he said, "You're welcome, Robbie."

As the boy ducked away, Ryder couldn't have stopped himself from looking over at Lindsay. Tears shimmered in her eyes, her soft mouth trembling, but Ryder didn't miss the shadows that seemed to creep up behind her smile.

Was she worried that he was getting too close to Robbie? As a single mom, and perhaps a slightly overprotective one at that, she would always have her son's best interest at heart. "Lindsay—"

"About time I get my kitchen back," Ellie sniffed, interrupting the moment as she joined them at the entrance to the small space.

Though she'd oohed and aahed over Lindsay's choices for the remodeling, once the demo disrupted her normal routine, Ellie hadn't been so appreciative. Each morning, Ryder overheard her complain that she always put on a pot of coffee first thing, and she'd been aghast when Lindsay suggested plugging the small appliance into an outlet in her bedroom and using water from the bathroom faucet. As if that water was somehow inferior to what would have come from the tap in the kitchen.

"How can I cook you and Robbie breakfast when I don't even have a stove and the refrigerator's sitting on the back porch? My refrigerator is *outside*, Lindsay."

In the face of her grandmother's agitation, Lindsay had been a study in calm, quiet patience. "It's only for a few days, Gran, and when Ryder's done you'll have a kitchen that will outshine the ones those celebrity chefs use on their television shows."

Ryder had hidden his smile, thinking that this was the Lindsay her coworkers saw in action every day. The PR expert putting the best spin on the situation.

"Almost, Ellie," he said to the older woman now. "I'll finish grouting this afternoon, and then the new appliances will all arrive tomorrow."

"Oh, all right. I've waited this long. I suppose another day won't hurt." She sighed, but Ryder hadn't missed the grin she fought to hide when he mentioned the new appliances.

That, too, had been a battle for Lindsay as Ellie insisted her antiquated dishwasher, oven and refrigerator were all perfectly fine. Only after Ryder lucked out and found a store with a demonstration kitchen, where customers could go in and try out the appliances for themselves, had Ellie changed her stubborn stance and actually upgraded to the state-of-the-art, stainless steel appliances.

Lindsay had frowned a little at the extravagance. "Well, we can always write it into the contract that the appliances aren't included with the house."

"Uh-huh," Ryder had agreed even though he couldn't help thinking the spin Lindsay was putting on her grandmother's house might end up backfiring. Once the remodeling was complete, why would Ellie want to leave? He had a feeling the diminutive gray-haired woman would be harder to budge than the ancient refrigerator on the back porch.

He was putting his money on Lindsay not being able to convince Ellie to move with a side bet that maybe, just maybe, Ellie would be the one to convince Lindsay to stay...

"I think this calls for a celebration," he said, "and as

Ellie has pointed out—numerous times—she can't cook without a kitchen, so I guess that means we'll have to go out to eat."

He'd expected an enthusiastic response, not the silence he received in answer instead. "Robbie? Not up for pizza?"

The boy glanced over at Lindsay and back again as he bit down on his lower lip. "Tyler and Brayden invited me over to spend the night. They're gonna download the new superhero movie."

"Well, I know I can't compete with a guy in a cape. Ladies, how about you?"

"Oh, I'm so sorry, Ryder," Ellie apologized, somewhat profusely, "but I have book club tonight."

"Book club is on Wednesday," Lindsay said, her eyes narrowing in a frown as she gazed at her grandmother.

"It moved," Ellie said with a smile. "So it looks like it'll be the two of you tonight. The perfect chance for you and Ryder to talk."

"The perfect chance for you and Ryder to talk."
For all of five minutes, that had been Lindsay's plan. She and Ryder would pick up pizza—not that she'd be able to swallow a single bite—come back to the house, and she would tell him about Robbie. But as they walked out, making plans for what time he'd come by, he'd caught her hand in his.

"Since it's just the two of us tonight," he said, his voice a lower, deeper murmur than when he'd suggested going out for pizza a few minutes earlier, "how about something a little fancier?"

Her pulse pounding a crazy beat Ryder could no doubt feel as he brushed his thumb along the tender inside of her wrist, Lindsay swallowed hard and fought for a teasing tone. "Burgers and fries?"

"Fancier," he said with a tug on her hand that drew her

closer. Her tennis shoes straddled his steel-toed boot, and the heat and hardness of his body tempted her to move even closer. "I was thinking more like a surf and turf, a nice bottle of wine and napkins that aren't made out of paper."

It was on the tip of Lindsay's tongue to make another lighthearted comment, but the masculine interest in his green gaze silenced her. "Are you—are you asking me out on a date?"

His lips twisted in a wry smile as he admitted, "I am, and quite badly, I suppose, if you have to ask."

"No, not badly at all. It's just…"

She'd been waiting fourteen years for Ryder Kincaid to ask her out on a date, and a part of Lindsay couldn't believe it was happening. "I'd love to go out with you, Ryder."

He'd smiled at her response, not the cocky grin of the boy who'd known he could have any girl, but the pleased expression of a man who'd gotten the answer he'd hoped for. "I'll pick you up at six."

Lindsay's heartbeat had tripped all over itself as she watched Ryder walk away. She'd waited until he drove off with a wave before running back upstairs and into the bathroom. She'd taken a long, hot shower, and by the time she stepped out onto the nubby pale blue shower mat, she was buffed and polished from head to toe.

She'd still been draped in a matching towel, drying her hair, when Robbie told her he was leaving. She'd said good-bye through the closed door and listened to the sound of his footsteps pounding down the stairs. She sensed Ellie waiting on the other side for a bit longer.

"You have to tell him, Lindsay," her grandmother said softly before she, too, went downstairs.

And she would.

"But not tonight," Lindsay whispered to her reflection as she focused on anchoring the small butterfly barrette above her right temple. The small, jeweled piece matched the print on the flared skirt she'd topped with a turquoise sweater. Ryder had said fancy, and she was taking him at his word.

A date with Ryder Kincaid.

The butterflies on her skirt might have been caught midflight, but the ones in her stomach started winging wildly in every direction when she heard the doorbell ring. She slipped on a pair of silver, strappy heels and rushed out of the bedroom. She was breathless by the time she opened the door, but it had little to do with the quick step down the stairs and everything to do with the man standing in front of her.

Since coming back, she'd seen Ryder in jeans and T-shirts suitable to the remodeling work he was doing. Nothing fancy, nothing to distract from the pure, 100 percent masculine appeal of his muscular arms, broad shoulders and long legs. She wouldn't have imagined he could possibly look sexier.

She should have known better.

His rich brown hair was combed back from his forehead, and the slate-blue dress shirt he swore made his eyes look almost impossibly green. He had one hand tucked into the pocket of his charcoal-colored slacks, a confident yet relaxed stance that had Lindsay's mouth drying out and watering all at the same time.

"You look amazing."

Ryder laughed, and Lindsay felt a slow flush start to climb from the scooped neckline of her sweater as he said, "Thank you, but I think that's supposed to be my line."

Instantly flustered, she stuttered, "Oh, I— You—"

"Let's try this again," he said as he held out the small bouquet of flowers in his right hand. "Thank you for coming out with me tonight, Lindsay. You look amazing."

"Oh, they're beautiful," she breathed as she lifted the mix of pink carnations, white daisies and purple irises to her nose. Along with the fresh, summery scent of the flowers, Lindsay caught a hint of Ryder's spicy aftershave, the combination almost enough to make her feel light-headed. "And thank you."

After placing the flowers in one of her grandmother's crystal vases, she grabbed a small, beaded bag and tried to hide her nerves as Ryder placed his hand on the small of her back and guided her out the door.

"So, where are we going?" Lindsay asked as he led her toward the passenger-side door of his truck. As much as she appreciated the gentlemanly gesture, she wished he wasn't watching so closely as she eyed the distance from the ground to the vehicle's running board. Especially when he seemed to enjoy her dilemma as she tried to subtly hike her skirt up far enough to make the climb.

The hint of a smile teased his lips as he answered, "A resort opened in Redfield a few years ago."

"Oh." Redfield was a forty-five-minute drive and far enough away that no one from Clearville was likely to see them together.

You're being ridiculous. This isn't high school anymore. Ryder isn't the cool kid afraid to hang with the book nerd.

And yet as Ryder closed the door and circled around to the driver's seat, Lindsay couldn't help thinking back to those days, to the reason why not a single soul in Clearville had ever suspected Ryder was Robbie's father. No one had ever seen them together. She'd tutored him in the back corner of the library, and on those occasions when he'd convinced her to play hooky...well, they hadn't wanted to get caught, had they? So they'd carefully slipped away without anyone noticing.

And on the night of Billy Cummings's party, a party she'd attended because she knew Ryder would be there and because she'd heard he'd broken up with Brittany, he'd found her alone on a swing set.

She'd barely lasted fifteen minutes inside the crowded house, where the loud music, louder voices and freely flowing alcohol had instantly overwhelmed her. She'd been bumped into three times, stepped on twice and had a beer spilled down her new sweater. It was the first party she'd attended her senior year—with graduation only weeks away—and she'd felt as awkward, out of place and miserable as she had the first day of high school.

"Have you been to this resort before?"

"No, that's why I thought it would be perfect." He kept his attention on the rearview mirror as he backed out of the driveway but glanced over and met her gaze before shifting gears. "A new place for a new start."

The promise in his green eyes—along with a hint of doubt as if he still questioned whether they would have this second chance—was enough for Lindsay to shove her own insecurities aside. "You're right. That does sound perfect."

Chapter Twelve

Ryder couldn't remember everything he and Lindsay talked about as they made the drive down Main Street, through the heart of Clearville and onto the two-lane highway that led out of town. The conversations switched from favorite books to favorite movies to taking turns hitting buttons on the radio as they searched for favorite songs, laughing when more often than not they came across a country-western station—one type of music neither of them could stand.

He flicked on the windshield wipers as a light mist started to fall, and Lindsay turned down the radio to listen to the sound of the storm. She told him about her parents, who were both teachers and had taken positions at the university, which had led them to move to Phoenix. She talked about her job and some of the pitfalls of working in PR. She talked about Robbie, the love filling her voice as strongly as an accent unique and belonging solely to Lindsay.

But she never talked about Robbie's father.

Ryder couldn't decide if the complete omission was deliberate or if Tony Pirelli was so far removed from her and Robbie's lives that he didn't deserve a mention. It wasn't that Ryder wanted to hear Lindsay go on about the man who'd once been such a big part of her life. He certainly had no desire to talk about Brittany. But he thought if Lindsay would talk about Tony—just once—then he would know. He'd be able to hear in her voice if she was still in love with the other man.

Ryder didn't want to believe that—didn't even want to think about it—but he could feel Lindsay holding back. Maybe it was because of their past. Maybe it was the uncertainty of their future.

Their conversation tapered off as the storm picked up, the sweep of the blades struggling to wipe the sheets of water from the windshield. Thunder rumbled in the distance, and flashes of lightning split the night sky. Ryder swore and swerved to the right as the headlights, barely piercing through the sheets of rain, illuminated a fallen tree limb in the middle of the road.

A loud thud ricocheted beneath the truck's undercarriage, and the steering wheel jerked in his hands. The tires lost traction with the pavement, hydroplaning off onto the shoulder of the road, close enough that low-hanging braches slapped against the windshield and passenger-side window.

He heard Lindsay gasp and wanted to reassure her, but his whole focus was on righting the vehicle and keeping it from slamming hood-first into a tree. Finally the tires regained their grip and the truck shuddered to a halt off the highway.

The windshield wipers and pounding rain were the only sounds until Ryder found his voice. "Are you okay?"

Lindsay nodded. "Fine, yes."

"I'm so sorry. That was—"

"Not your fault. I didn't see that branch until it was right in front of us, either. You missed the biggest part."

"Yeah, I know I caught a piece of it, though." Shifting into gear, he stepped on the gas and immediately felt the truck pull to one side. No wonder the vehicle had felt so unresponsive. "We've got a flat."

He was already reaching for the door when Lindsay placed a hand on his arm. "Ryder, wait! It's pouring out there. Shouldn't we…call someone instead?"

"Probably won't get cell service this far out of town. Besides, I can change a tire. It'll only take a few minutes."

Of course, it only took a few seconds for him to be soaked to the skin. He'd grabbed a flashlight and some flares from the emergency kit he kept on hand, but the dim glow and the constant stream of water running down his face made the working conditions almost impossible. Add in the mud soaking into his shoes and the knees of his pants as he maneuvered the jack into place, and he was downright miserable.

He swore as the tire iron slipped off the lug nut as he caught sight of movement from the corner of his eye. Gorgeous legs…and bare feet. He looked up just as Lindsay angled an umbrella to shield them both from the worst of the rain. "I found this behind the seat," she called over the loud pounding of water against nylon.

He hadn't bothered to take the umbrella, knowing he wouldn't have been able to hold on to it while changing the tire. But he hadn't expected—

"Lindsay, get back in the truck! You're getting soaked! And where the hell are your shoes!"

"Inside. I didn't want them to get wet. Hand me the flashlight. I'll hold it so you can actually see what you're doing." Sensing another argument coming, she said, "Like you said, I'm already getting soaked. Too late now, so you might as well accept my help."

Her skirt and sweater had already molded to her body, the material becoming almost translucent, outlining every detail from the curve of her thighs, the subtle flare of her hips, the delicate shape of her breasts… A slight shiver shook her body as he lifted his gaze to meet hers, and while Ryder would have liked to believe the sexual tension arcing between them was the cause, he wasn't taking any chances.

Handing her the flashlight, he promised, "Five minutes."

Ryder wasn't sure if he made his time frame, but he worked fast enough to do a pit crew proud. Even so, he was a muddy mess and Lindsay was trembling head to toe by the time they climbed back into the cab.

He cranked the heat on high, pointing all the vents in her direction. "Here. See if this helps."

"That's good. I'm good," she insisted even though her teeth were still chattering.

He had reached for the controls again when Lindsay gasped and caught his wrist. "You're hurt."

He looked down, a little surprised to see how badly he'd scraped his knuckles when the tire iron slipped. Blood welled along the broken skin, and the slight swelling would likely lead to a colorful bruise by morning. "It's nothing," he protested, his voice a little gruffer than he'd intended.

But the simple touch of her hands against his skin heated Ryder's blood until the inside of the truck felt like a sauna. Rain-soaked and shivering, she was still the most beautiful woman he'd ever seen. And maybe part of that beauty was *because* she was rain-soaked and shivering.

Most women he knew would have been complaining about the missed reservations and the time they'd wasted getting ready to go out for what ended up being a ruined evening. None of them would have set foot into the storm to hold the umbrella and flashlight for him.

Ryder swore beneath his breath, and Lindsay froze as she dabbed at his knuckles with a tissue.

"Am I hurting you?

"What? No." Too frustrated to even acknowledge the stinging scrape on his hand, he ground out, "I…I wanted this date to be perfect."

Her focus still on his hand, her damp hair falling forward to shield her face, Lindsay murmured, "It is perfect."

He must have misheard her. Maybe the rain pounding down on the truck or the rumbling thunder drowned out the words she'd actually said. "Perfect? How can you possibly call this perfect?"

"Because I'm on a date with you."

The soft words slammed into him with more force than if the truck had run headlong into one of the redwoods lining the road. Sincerity and longing swirled in her blue-green gaze as she glanced up at him, and Ryder forgot about the cut on his hand. Forgot about the rain pounding down around them, forgot they were pulled over on the side of the highway.

All that mattered was Lindsay and that look in her eyes and the quiet words that sent anticipation and urgency pounding through his veins. "Lindsay."

Whatever else he might have said was lost as he claimed her mouth with his own. As he spoke his desire with the brush of his lips, as he pleaded his case with the stroke of his tongue and sang her praises as she welcomed him inside. The softness, the sweetness, the promise of more had him groaning low in his throat as she buried her hands in his damp hair. Her fingers were cool and trembling but still so expressive in her demand.

He shifted to pull her close, the bucket seats and steering wheel a detriment he overcame by reaching down to shove the seat back. He lifted Lindsay into his lap without breaking contact with the kiss. The soft, warm weight of her pressed against him, and his hips instinctively jerked. The damp material of their clothes hardly seemed like any kind of barrier as her breasts brushed against his chest with every gasping breath.

Her head fell back as his kiss trailed down the side of her neck, her skin rainwater fresh and silky smooth…

"You smell like strawberries," he murmured at the hollow of her throat.

"Lotion." The muscles there pulled and contracted against his lips as she swallowed and forced the words out. "It's lotion."

Sweeter than perfume and so much more arousing as Ryder imagined Lindsay smoothing the creamy moisture over every inch of skin. It was a path he followed with his own hands—from her neck, to the points of her shoulders, to the gentle swell of her breasts and nipples as lush and mouthwatering as any summer-ripe fruit.

She arched her back, pressing herself more firmly into his palms—and then nearly jumped out of her skin at the sudden blare of a horn.

"Oh! Sorry, I must have hit—"

The steering wheel. Ryder's jaw tightened as he swore beneath his breath. She'd hit the freaking steering wheel because they were in his truck, groping through each other's clothing, rushing like a couple of teenagers when he had sworn—*sworn*—that if he had a second chance with Lindsay, he would do this right.

Lindsay pushed her damp hair behind one ear and glanced longingly at the passenger seat as if she could somehow transport herself there without having to shift and slide and use his body to lever away from him. The shoulders she'd thrown back with such abandon were curved inward now as if trying to protect herself from a blow to the heart.

"Sorry," she said again. "Guess that kind of broke the mood, didn't it?"

"Lindsay." He curved his fingers into her hips, holding her still when what he really wanted was to pull her closer, to feel the softness of her pressed against his arousal... To show her how easily, how completely, she turned him on. But if he did, he feared he wouldn't stop. That even though they weren't teenagers anymore, she could still make him feel like one...

He said her name again and waited until she looked at him—wide-eyed with uncertainty. "We're not eighteen anymore," he reminded her and saw the faint blush rise to her skin as she remembered the last time they'd been parked in a car like this. "I want you, but I want more than five minutes of fumbling through two layers of clothes."

He grimaced a little at his own bluntly honest assessment of their only other time together. Lindsay deserved more. So much more. They both did. And that thought alone gave him the willpower to carefully set her away from him but not before he stole one more heated kiss.

"I want you," he murmured against her lips. "I want you...and I want a bed...and I want all night."

Faint streaks of daylight were edging around the curtains by the time Lindsay opened her eyes. With Ryder's arm curved possessively around her waist and his warm, strong body running the length of hers, leaving was the last thing she wanted to do.

She closed her eyes for another minute, breathing in the faint scent of his aftershave on the sheets and steeping herself in memories.

He'd kept his promise the night before, taking his time, his lovemaking so slow and so seductive...Lindsay had thought she would go out of her mind with wanting and loved every minute of it. She barely remembered the ride back to his place and had no more than a brief image of a darkened living room and hallway before he led her to his bedroom.

The faint glow from a bedside table filled the room, but it was Ryder's words that had lit her from the inside out as he murmured, "I want to see you. I want to see everything I missed ten years ago."

And for a split second, the fear, the worry, the guilt over everything he had missed for the past ten years clutched at her heart with cold, icy fingers. But then it was Ryder's hands on her—warm and arousing—as he unbuttoned her sweater one tiny pearl at a time, stopping every inch along the way to press a kiss on the skin he revealed. The hollow of her throat, the valley between her breasts, the indentation at her navel... She'd been breathless, dizzy, by the time he reached the final button, and he still would not be hurried.

Her skirt was next, a slow damp slide as he slipped his hands beneath the elastic waistband, the material bunching at his wrists as he trailed his palms down her outer thighs. Goose bumps rose in the wake of his touch, tiny markers that seemed to say *Ryder Kincaid was here*.

His eyes glowed as he took in her lacy teal bra and panties. "Why am I not surprised?" he murmured. "Even your underwear matches your outfits."

"Not always."

"Ah, no fair. Now you're just teasing me, knowing that every time I look at you, I'll be wondering what you're wearing under your fancy clothes."

Emboldened by the heat in his eyes, she said, "Because you weren't wondering already?"

His husky laughter sent shivers down her spine. "You're

right, but now I'll know how sexy you look in them…and out of them."

But sexy, Lindsay decided as he kissed her again, wasn't about how she looked—in or out of her clothes. It was in how he made her feel as he laid her on the bed and covered her naked body with his own. As he kissed her and touched her until her heart cried out for more, until her hips were rising to meet his thrusts, until the pleasure broke over her as she called out his name…

Pressure built in her chest, and her quick, inhaled breath was loud in the silence of the room.

How many years had she longed to feel Ryder's arms wrapped around her? To have him look at her the way he had done the night before as if she were the only woman in the world? The only woman in *his* world?

It should have been perfect. It should have been a dream come true. Instead she felt everything she'd ever wanted was just outside her grasp, and the more she tried to hang on, the farther it slipped from her desperate, scrambling reach.

She was falling in love with him. Falling in love with a man she'd been lying to for ten years.

The longer she waited to tell the truth, the more it would hurt, but knowing that only made her want to put off telling the truth even longer…

Carefully pushing the covers aside, Lindsay tried to slide from the bed.

"Where are you going?" Ryder's rasping voice scraped across her nerve endings, scattering goose bumps over her skin.

"To get Robbie."

His arm tightened, pulling her back against his body. "Robbie's not here," he argued reasonably.

Lindsay managed a soft laugh. "Yes, I know. He's at

your brother and sister-in-law's, and I have to go pick him up this morning."

"Not this early, you don't. Trust me, if my brother's half as smart as I think he is, he and Nina are taking advantage of the kids sleeping in after staying up too late watching movies and eating junk food."

"I want to get back before Ellie wakes up." Her grandmother wouldn't have waited up, as she rarely made it past nine o'clock, but she was an early riser. "It probably sounds hopelessly old-fashioned—"

"You're staying in your grandmother's house and you want to be respectful. I wouldn't expect anything less."

As it turned out, Lindsay didn't have to pick Robbie up that morning. By the time she got back to Ellie's, snuck upstairs for a shower and came down in time to help her grandmother with breakfast as if it were any other day, Robbie called to ask if he could hang out with the Kincaid boys a little longer.

"Sounds like he had a good time last night," Ellie said as she handed Lindsay a bowl of cold cereal with a frown. "I'm sure he's having a more nutritious breakfast than we are."

"Whatever he's having is fine. And so is this. Believe it or not, I do not need waffles, pancakes, bacon and eggs or some combination of the above for breakfast every morning. I'll have gained fifteen pounds by the time I go back…"

Lindsay's voice trailed off as she shoved a spoonful of flaky cereal into her mouth one sentence too late.

"You didn't tell him, did you?" Ellie stated as she took a seat across from Lindsay at the dining room table.

Lindsay chewed for as long as she possibly could before shaking her head as she reached for her glass of milk. "Not yet."

"Lindsay…"

Dropping her spoon into the bowl, she protested, "I know, okay? I know everything you're going to say, because it's the same thing I've been telling myself for days. I have to tell him. Waiting will only make it harder. He's going to hate me when he finds out the truth…"

She lowered her gaze, but her voice had already broken on the sharp ache in her throat, so what good did it do to try to hide her tears?

"Oh. Lindsay. He's not going to hate you."

"You can't know that."

"I've seen the way he looks at you, too. He cares for you."

"But after I tell him about Robbie—"

"He'll be angry, and it will take time for him to get over that, but he will. For Robbie's sake. You'll see."

Lindsay didn't doubt Ryder would love their son. And that would have to be enough, because as much as she wanted to hold on to hope, she couldn't imagine Ryder feeling the same way about her once she told him the truth.

Chapter Thirteen

Laughter spilled over the fence from the Kincaids' back-yard as Lindsay pulled the back gate open. Nerves danced in her stomach at the thought of seeing Ryder again so soon after seeing him naked. She resisted the urge to wipe at her forehead, sure the words *I spent the night with Ryder Kincaid* were stamped there for all to see.

But her small smile at the thought quickly disappeared as she thought of the other, even more telling words she had yet to reveal.

Ryder Kincaid's the father of my child.

Was she fooling herself by clinging to her grandmother's words? By putting her hope in the idea that Ryder might be falling for her, too? If she could nurture these new, precious feelings for a while longer, was it possible that he would grow to care enough for her to understand why she'd kept Robbie a secret?

Or was she only being selfish, trying to hold on to what

they had for as long as she could, knowing that once she told the truth, she'd have no choice but to let Ryder go?

Her heart ached at the thought and then a little more at the sight of him standing by his brother near the outdoor grill. He looked so good, far more mouthwatering in baggy tan cargo shorts and a white T-shirt than whatever Bryce was cooking up for dinner.

With his bronzed, muscled limbs on display, he looked so undeniably masculine, so unbelievably gorgeous, it was all Lindsay could do not to race across the lush green grass, throw herself into his arms and—

"Hey, Lins."

She stopped short at the offhand greeting, at the casual smile and nod. "Ryder..." Her voice trailed off as he'd already turned away, back to where his brother was manning the grill.

"Hi, Mom!" Robbie rushed over to greet her, surprising her with a quick hug.

Swallowing against the unease churning in her stomach, she wrapped her arm around his shoulders. "Hey, Robbie. How was the movie?"

"Awesome!" he exclaimed with a fist pump that would do a superhero proud. "And then we played video games and stayed up late—uh, but not too late."

"Oh, of course not," Lindsay said wryly.

"And Tyler's mom says we can stay over for dinner. Can we?"

"Oh, I don't know," she hedged.

"You should stay," Bryce called out as he greeted her with a wave of his tongs.

"Please," Nina said as she carried plates out toward the picnic tables, "as the lone female, I'm seriously outnumbered here."

"Please, Mom..."

"Okay," Lindsay agreed, although she couldn't help noticing Ryder hadn't said anything at all. "Is there anything I can do to help?"

"There are some cans of soda in the fridge if you want to bring those out," Nina said.

Lindsay nodded, grateful to keep busy especially with an errand that would give her a moment to herself. Slipping into the kitchen, she leaned against the back door and tried to swallow around the lump in her throat. Ryder hadn't just blown her off, had he? The backyard was filled with family members, including his nephews and Robbie, so she certainly hadn't anticipated the same greeting as if they'd been alone. But she'd still expected some kind of acknowledgment that their relationship had changed, that last night had meant something to him.

Tears burned her eyes, but she wouldn't let them fall. Not this time.

Pushing away from the door, she headed for the refrigerator and the drinks inside. She took a moment to press one of the cans against her heated face before setting it on the counter. She was bending toward the bottom shelf for two more when the door softly clicked shut behind her.

She turned as Ryder reached out, pulling her into his arms and nearly off her feet. One of the cold cans slipped from her grasp, hit the hardwood floor with a thud and rolled across the kitchen.

"Ryder! What—" The started exclamation was swallowed as he claimed her mouth in a heated kiss designed to leave her hungry and longing for more.

Her lips were tingling and her breath ragged against her throat when Ryder broke away. Feeling very much the victim of a kiss-and-run, she stuttered, "What…what was that?"

His forehead still pressed to hers he said, "That was me dying to kiss you from the moment you walked into the backyard."

"But you didn't— I mean, earlier—"

"I love my family, don't get me wrong, but they can be nosy pains in the ass sometimes. I don't want them making too big a deal out of this."

"Oh, sure. Right," Lindsay agreed, a little hollowly as his words sucked out the joy she'd felt when she thought the two of them making love *was* a big deal.

"You're the first woman I've dated since the divorce. Hell, you're the first woman I've dated other than Brittany since...ever. I just want to take things slow."

"Slow..." She gave a small laugh. "I'm not entirely sure how that word applies to a relationship that includes sex on a first date."

Ryder frowned as his hands slid from her shoulders, and he took a small step back. "Are you sorry we—"

Lindsay shook her head. "No, I'm not sorry." She'd taken a chance and made her own decision. She wasn't going to beat herself up over it now. "Like you said, no big deal."

"That's not what I meant."

"It's what you said, Ryder."

"Okay, fine." Crossing his arms over his chest, he demanded, "Are you taking the job at the Chamber of Commerce?"

"What?"

"Are you and Robbie moving back to Clearville? Are you going to keep living with Ellie? Will you be looking for a new house here? Have you toured the school, met with Robbie's new teachers? Have you—"

"No, I— Ryder, stop!"

Relaxing his stance, he said, "That's a small sample of the questions that would be going through my brother's and sister-in-law's heads if they knew we were together. They might not come straight out and ask, but I know it's what they'd be thinking. And we could try to put them off by saying we're just dating and that it's just casual, but my brother knows me too well to fall for that. Too well not to realize I'm falling for you."

Lindsay's breath caught on a quick, startled inhale. "Oh."

"And I know you don't have the answers to any of those questions, so I'd rather keep our relationship between the two of us until you do."

Ryder was falling for her.

After over ten years of loving him…

After over ten years of lying to him.

Lindsay didn't blame him for holding back, for keeping their relationship undefined and under wraps. Was she staying in Clearville? Was she going back to Phoenix? She couldn't make that decision until she told Ryder he was Robbie's father.

But every time she tried, she remembered the look on his face when they stood in his brother's kitchen, the sincerity in his voice as he spoke the words she never thought she'd hear, and she…couldn't.

And the longer she waited, the deeper the truth got buried beneath her own growing feelings. Like a sleepwalker clinging to a dream world, she kept her eyes closed to the reality of the steep cliffs ahead.

So she pretended not to see the disappointed, telling looks her grandmother gave her. Pretended not to notice the little details of how Robbie had taken to mimicking Ryder's habit of standing with his hands in his back pockets, his feet spread wide and head cocked at a slight angle. Or to think about what it meant that Robbie had asked for a baseball cap after Ryder had worn one while refinishing the wooden floors in Ellie's living room. A hat she hadn't had the chance to buy before Ryder brought one over the next day.

The boy's eyes had widened behind his glasses, and he'd thrown his arms around Ryder in a quick hug before slipping the cap over his dark blond hair. Backward, the way Ryder wore his…

"What about this one? Lindsay? Lindsay?"

She blinked as Ryder waved a shade of blue paint sample in front of her face. "Sorry, my mind drifted for a second. What were you saying?"

"I was asking what you thought of this color for your grandmother's living room, but then your eyes glazed over, which either means you don't like blue or the whole remodeling process is starting to take its toll."

"I'm fine, and blue's fine. That one's nice," she said as she pointed to a Wedgwood blue in the middle of the light to dark range.

"Are you sure? Because there are about a million or so other shades," he said as he gestured to the paint displays lining an entire aisle at the home improvement store, "and you don't have to choose one right now. There's still time."

Time but not much time. Lindsay's hands tightened on the shopping cart handle. She knew based on the schedule he'd given her at the start of the job that painting would be one of the last projects, and she wondered how long she could put off picking a color…

"What do you think of this?" she asked, reaching for a sample roughly the shade of a traffic cone.

"Seriously?"

"Or maybe this one," she suggested, grabbing a bloodred square.

"Definitely suffering from remodeling overload."

"Or how about—"

Ryder caught her wrist before she could make another inappropriate selection and pulled her into his arms. "How about we save this for another time and play hooky today instead?"

"That sounds like the perfect cure."

"Hey, Lindsay," a female voice called out.

She turned in time to see Cherrie Macintosh pushing a cart down the aisle. "Oh, Cherrie, hi."

Brittany's best friend eyed the arm Ryder had wrapped around Lindsay's waist and greeted him with a cool nod. "Ryder. I heard you were back in town."

"Cherrie. How have you been?"

"Busy, you know, with the reunion coming up this weekend. It's going to be a great time, but I don't think I saw your names on the RSVP list." Her finely arched eyebrows rose in question.

Ryder hadn't moved his arm from around Lindsay's waist even though Cherrie was one of the biggest gossips around, and Lindsay found herself holding her breath—

"Sorry, Cherrie. My sister's coming to visit, and I'm picking her up at the airport that night."

"Oh, well," the blonde said almost dismissively before turning to Lindsay with an eager smile. "How about you, Lindsay? It would be great to catch up after all this time, to hear about your job in Phoenix. Patricia Bennett says you've been on television."

Lindsay didn't dare glance in Ryder's direction. She could sense the laughter he was trying to hold back and had to admit the role reversal was almost funny. Suddenly Ryder was on the outside looking in and Lindsay was one of the cool kids, getting invited to the party.

"I'm, um, not sure, Cherrie, but I'll let you know."

"Okay, then. I've gotta go. The store's doing an irrigation how-to demo out in the landscaping department in a few minutes."

"Irrigation?" Lindsay echoed.

Waving a pink-tipped manicured hand, Cherrie offered, "What can I say? Some of the guys who work here are hot."

"Well, she sure hasn't changed much," Ryder said wryly as the blonde sashayed off in search of demonstrative hot guys.

"Oh, I don't know. She's a lot nicer than I remember."

"You know, if you want to go to the reunion, I could see if someone else could pick up Sydney. The rest of the family's going to an out-of-town swim meet for the boys, but maybe—"

"No, you don't have to change your plans just because I've changed my mind about going."

Looking a bit skeptical, he asked, "You really want to go?"

"I do."

Not because Cherrie Macintosh thought she was worth getting to know now that she'd been on television or because she had anything to prove to the rest of her classmates. Lindsay wanted to prove to herself that she really had changed from the shy girl in high school. The one who had sat at home during every homecoming dance, every spring fling, every prom during those years.

But as big a moment as it would be for Lindsay to walk into the reunion alone, she still wished she would be walking in with Ryder at her side.

Chapter Fourteen

"Thanks again for picking me up," Sydney said about an hour into the ninety-minute drive from the airport, "especially when there's someplace you'd rather be."

Ryder glanced over at the passenger seat, where his younger sister gazed at him with a knowing expression. "I never said I had other plans."

"No, but you keep glancing at your watch, and Nina told me your high school reunion is tonight."

"And I told Nina and Bryce I wasn't planning to go."

Ryder didn't know what to think about Sydney's visit home. She seemed to be trying too hard to convince him and the rest of the family that everything was fine. Which, considering that Sydney was the peacemaker who always wanted everyone to get along, was enough to make Ryder believe the exact opposite was true.

"But since I caught an earlier flight, you'll have plenty of time to go home and get your sexy on."

"Yeah, that's just what I'm going to do."

"You should! You know you want to. To have the chance
to relive your glory days as Clearville High's star quarterback, prom king, most likely to succeed…"

That was the very reason he *hadn't* wanted to attend the
reunion. Last thing he'd wanted was to fake a smile while
his "good friends" rubbed in how spectacularly he hadn't
succeeded—not in college ball or in the NFL as he'd once
dreamed. But ever since Lindsay said she'd changed her
mind about attending the reunion, going didn't sound like
such a bad idea. Not for a chance to relive the past, but for
another opportunity to grab hold of right now and spend
the time with Lindsay.

Time that was growing short if she chose to go back to
Phoenix. As much as he wanted her to make up her mind,
to decide to take the job at the Chamber of Commerce, to
stay in Clearville, those were huge, life-altering decisions,
not only for her but also for Robbie. She'd be taking a huge
chance while he…he wouldn't have to risk a thing. He'd
already made the move back, already had a job he enjoyed
and was surrounded by family.

No, if he wanted Lindsay to take a chance on him—on
them—he needed to be the one putting his heart on the line.

And he couldn't think of a better placed to do that than
their high school reunion.

"Ryder Kincaid. Why am I not surprised to see you
here after all?" Cherrie Macintosh shook her head, but her
smile was more than a little smug as he walked through
the double doors into Hillcrest House's elegant ballroom.

Ryder wasn't sure what had changed the woman's attitude since seeing him at the home improvement store
three days earlier, but he didn't really care. He glanced at
the group of people gathered near a welcoming table set up
by the doorway, but he didn't see Lindsay's honey-brown
head among them. He'd thought about surprising her by

picking her up for the night, but then decided it would be even more of a surprise if he showed up unannounced at the reunion.

He couldn't wait to see her, to catch sight of the look on her face when she spotted him from across the ballroom...

"Guess I know what changed your mind, don't I?" Cherrie was saying.

He'd seen more than a few familiar faces, classmates who greeted him with waves, a few who came over to shake his hand, slap him on the back or kiss his cheek. Ryder smiled through it all, his impatience growing. He didn't know why Cherrie had stuck close, but he'd take any help he could get.

Lindsay was the reason he'd changed his mind, and if the other woman could help him find her, then dressing up in his suit and tie left over from his days in San Francisco and suffering through half a dozen conversations that all started with the words *remember when* would all be worth it.

"You'll love this," Cherrie was saying. "We hired a photographer and set up a raised dais and floral arch exactly like the one we had at prom. It's perfect, right? To relive that moment ten years later."

Ryder had no interest in recapturing that night or any other night from the past. He wanted to focus on the here and now, on sharing this night with Lindsay. But as he caught sight of the white arched trellis, of the light pink carnations and silver ribbons woven through and cascading down the sides, as he saw the woman in a red dress standing near the circular platform—

His heart stopped, but instead of skipping forward to pick up the pace, instead of pounding inside his chest and urging him on, it sank to the pit of his stomach. Because the woman standing near the dais wasn't Lindsay.

It was his ex-wife, Brittany.

* * *

Lindsay sucked in a deep lungful of air as she stepped through Hillcrest's elegant entryway. As breathtaking as the coffered ceilings, crystal chandeliers and gleaming hardwood floors were, she could barely focus on the beautiful surroundings. Nerves snapped beneath her skin to the point where she almost expected to see electricity spark as her foot brushed across the richly patterned rug.

A member of the staff offered her a polite smile and said, "The reunion is being held in the ballroom to your left."

Thanking the young woman, Lindsay forced one foot in front of the other. She could do this. She'd handled far more difficult situations to let something as simple as a small-town high school reunion shake her confidence. She held her head high, her shoulders back and her spine straight. She even smiled a little as she recalled the hours she'd spent practicing until she could walk in the highest of heels without stumbling. Tonight, she wore rhinestone-studded pumps to match her strapless, pale gold dress, and her footsteps didn't falter even once as she walked down the hallway.

A rectangular table draped in a light pink tablecloth and swags of silver ribbon had been set up inside the ballroom's double doors. The woman manning the table waved a hand at the name tags spread across the surface. "The tags are in alphabetical order by last name, but you'll probably spot your picture first. Isn't that a great idea? To have everyone's senior picture on the name tag, so it's easy to remember who we used to be?"

"Great," Lindsay echoed. She'd always hated her senior picture. Hated almost every picture from high school, where her hair had been a frizzy mess and thick-framed glasses overwhelmed every other feature.

Picking up the name tag, Lindsay stared back at the girl

she'd once been. She'd worn her hair pulled back from her face that day, containing some of the curl, and she wasn't wearing her glasses. She'd forgotten that she started trying out contacts those last few months before graduation. A touch of mascara, blush and lipstick, applied with a slightly immature hand, highlighted her features as she gazed at the camera with a shy smile.

She didn't look geeky or awkward or unattractive. She simply looked...young.

And Lindsay managed a smile in return as she peeled off the backing and applied the name tag to her dress. As she stepped into the ballroom, she heard a few catcalls above the decade-old music beating from the speakers and glanced over at a circular platform in the corner. A camera flashed, capturing a man in a charcoal-gray suit and a woman draped in scarlet wrapped in each other's arms beneath a floral archway.

No, not a man and a woman. Lindsay reeled as the patterned carpet tilted beneath her feet.

Ryder...and Brittany.

With half his former classmates watching the spectacle as the photographer instructed him to place his arms around his ex's waist in a classic "prom picture pose," Ryder bared his teeth in a smile.

Had he thought even for a moment that his ex would attend the reunion, he would have stayed away. Hell, he should have walked away the minute he caught sight of her.

But then the photographer overheard that he and Brittany had been the prom king and queen from a decade earlier and pressed for a photo beneath the floral trellis.

And when Ryder had balked, Brittany had tossed her dark hair over her shoulder and met his gaze with a challenging smile. "Come on, Ryder. It's tradition, you know that."

Ryder hadn't wanted this night to have anything to do with the past, but he had too much pride to walk away. To let Brittany think she could still get under his skin.

Behind his gritted smile, he demanded, "What are you doing here, Brittany?"

Tilting her face toward his, she said, "It's my reunion, too, Ryder. You aren't the only one who gets to relive the glory days."

He couldn't swallow the snort of laughter. "You hated it here and swore you'd never set foot in this town again. You couldn't wait to get back to San Francisco."

"There was a time when you felt the same. A time when we felt the same way about so many things, remember?" She moved closer than the photographer had instructed, pressing her breasts against his side, and he felt…nothing.

Nothing but a wave of relief—like letting go of a heavy load he'd carried far too long—as he was finally over her. After fourteen years of making up, breaking up and making up again—

"Not anymore," he answered her.

"So you're really planning to stay here, then? In this nowheresville town?"

"Clearville's my home."

"It always was, wasn't it?" she said with a touch of bitterness. "Even all those years we were in San Francisco. I thought after being back here for almost a year, after everything you gave up, maybe you'd changed your mind. Maybe you would want to give us a second chance."

"A second chance?" The words sounded as incredulous coming from his own lips as they had coming from Brittany's.

His ex must have heard it, too, because she met his astounded gaze with a glare. "Yes! A second chance to have the life we'd always dreamed about—the high-profile, successful careers, the parties with the San Francisco elite…"

"That was your dream, Brittany. Not mine. Money, fame, fortune..." He shook his head. That dream had died a slow, painful death during endless football games spent on the sidelines and in punishing scrimmages on the practice squad. "I wanted more than that. I wanted a home, a *family*." He stressed the word, and Brittany had the grace to flush as her gaze cut away from his.

When that dream, too, died after a long-distance, gut-wrenching phone call from Brittany, he'd let his own dreams slip away. Following hers had been easier, safer even, and maybe that did make the unhappiness, the emptiness of their marriage, partly his fault.

"That's what I figured out once I heard you were seeing Lindsay Brookes." Brittany's lips twisted in a grimace. "House in the country, a big yard, kids... It's all yours, Ryder. I hope you're happy."

Her words were more sarcastic than sincere, but Ryder said, "I am happy."

Coming back to Clearville, spending time with Robbie and falling in love with Lindsay had opened his eyes to what he really wanted, to what a part of him had always wanted.

"Okay, here's to Clearville High's king and queen," the photographer called. "One more shot. Let's make it a good one!"

Her lips twisted in a smile, Brittany said, "You heard the man, Ryder. Let's make it good."

Before he knew what she planned, before the bright flash of the camera, she kissed him. An all-for-show mockery of a kiss that had Ryder wanting to wipe his mouth the moment it ended.

Amid catcalls and whistles from the people gathered around the dais, he gritted out the words beneath clenched teeth. "What the hell, Britt?"

"Might as well give folks around here *something* to

talk about," she said with a satisfied smile as she glanced over his shoulder.

And even before he turned, he knew what he would see—the look on Lindsay's face as he spotted her from across the ballroom. He swore beneath his breath as the color drained from her features, leaving frozen shock and icy fury behind. "Lindsay—"

She'd spun from the room before her name left his lips. As his foot hit the dais's first step, he heard Brittany give a short laugh behind him. "That's right, Ryder. Go running after little Lindsay. You always did have a thing for her."

And for the first time, he wondered if he hadn't been as careful as he'd thought about keeping that one night a secret. But none of that mattered anymore. He was done hiding his feelings for Lindsay.

He brushed by people in the crowded ballroom, catching up with her as she slipped out the front door and into the cool night air. "Lindsay, wait!"

Her high heels clicked along the cobblestone path cutting through the thick lawn toward the parking lot behind the towering Victorian. "Leave me alone, Ryder."

Reaching out, he caught her by the elbow and pulled her to a stop. "It's not what you think!"

"Oh, I know exactly what this is. Been there, done that, should have been smart enough not to fall for it a second time." Her eyes glittered as she gave a bitter, broken laugh. "Doesn't seem to matter, does it? Whether you and Brittany break up before senior prom or get divorced ten years later, all it takes is one crook of her finger, and you're back in her arms again."

"Brittany and I are not getting back together! I had no idea she would even be here tonight, and that kiss—that was all Brittany looking to be the center of attention. Do you really think that I'd—"

"What? Sleep with me and then go back to her?" The

sharp words lashed out, striking their mark, and he sucked in a deep breath.

His hand fell away from her arm. "For all that talk about second chances, you're never going to give me one, are you? I made a mistake ten years ago—a huge, horrible mistake—and no matter what I do or say now, when you look at me, that mistake is all you're ever going to see. Isn't it, Lindsay?"

Tipping her head back, she closed her eyes. Her beautiful features looked pale and fragile, her graceful neck, her slender shoulders and the gentle swell of her breasts above the gold bodice of her dress alabaster smooth in the moonlight. "A huge, horrible mistake," she echoed.

Ryder swore. "I didn't mean that night. I didn't mean *us*. I was talking about everything that came after."

"Yes, everything…" She opened her eyes, but she wasn't looking at him, gazing instead into a past neither of them could change. "I want to forgive you, Ryder. I want *you* to—" Lindsay shook her head. "But maybe it's too much to think we could start over."

"I don't believe that. I won't believe that, and I don't think you do, either. I don't think you would have made love with me the other night if you didn't think we at least have a chance to make this work."

"Seeing you with Brittany again…"

"I'm not with her. I came here tonight to be with you."

"But the two of you were together for so long." Off the cobblestone path, a stone bench, bleached white in the soft moonlight, sat nestled amid a trio of carefully sculpted topiary. Lindsay sank onto the seat, her uplifted gaze pleading with him to understand.

The last thing Ryder wanted to do was talk about his ex, but he couldn't ignore the unspoken question behind Lindsay's words. "You're right. By the time Brittany and I left for college, we'd already been a couple for four years.

Our entire senior year, all we talked about was getting out of Clearville and going to school together. We'd planned for it for so long that it felt like a done deal. Something that couldn't possibly change. At first, everything was good. We were two kids from a small town in a big city, and it actually made us closer. We started planning for the future again—this time for a big wedding as soon as we graduated."

He gave a rough laugh as he dropped onto the bench beside Lindsay. "You know, funny thing is, I never even asked her to marry me. Not really. Not the whole get-down-on-one-knee, big declaration of love with hearts and flowers and a ring… More like everyone just assumed it would happen after we graduated. The summer before our senior year, Brittany picked out the ring she wanted, and she and her mother started making all these plans.

"Don't get me wrong. I'm not saying it was all her fault we ended up like we did. But we'd been together for so long that it seemed like getting married was what we were supposed to do. Any doubts I had, well, that was just cold feet, right?"

"So, what happened to make you think it was more than cold feet?" Lindsay asked.

She had always read him so easily. The one girl who wouldn't put up with his BS. And if he hadn't screwed up their friendship, he couldn't help thinking things would have turned out so differently. "The wedding plans were in full force all through our last year of college. Before long, the ceremony and reception were becoming more important than the marriage, more important than our relationship. I tried telling myself that that was normal, too. Maybe Brittany was nervous like I was, and focusing on having the biggest, most elaborate wedding imaginable was her way of coping.

"But then Bryce and Nina came to visit with the boys.

Their youngest was a few months old at the time. Seeing the way Bryce looked at those boys, the way he looked at Nina…the love between them was like this tangible presence, something you could reach out and touch."

Ryder hadn't wanted to admit he'd been jealous, but the feeling was there, leaving him off balance and on edge. "After they left to go back home, Brittany made some comment about 'poor Nina' being stuck at home with two crying kids. We ended up getting into this huge fight. I'd always wanted kids and assumed Brittany felt the same. But it was kind of like our engagement. I'd never actually asked Brittany to marry me, and she never came right out and said she wanted a family. She said 'someday' and 'when we're ready.' But actions speak louder than words, and not once during Bryce and Nina's visit had she asked to hold Brayden.

"I told her I thought we needed to take a break, to really think about being married and not just about *getting* married. I thought she'd come unglued. I was totally shocked when she agreed. I should have known it was too easy. If I'd learned anything in all the years we were together, it should have been that life with Brittany was never that easy."

"So what happened? If you were that close to calling off the wedding…"

Night sounds filled the air—the chirp of a cricket, the whisper of wind through the trees, the faint rush of the surf against the rocky beach—as Ryder searched for the words he'd never spoken out loud. "A few weeks later, she told me she was pregnant."

"Pregnant!"

"Pregnant," he said, his voice sounding hollow from the pain and emptiness he still felt inside. "I knew then that I had to go through with the wedding. It was the right thing to do."

Out of the corner of his eye, he saw Lindsay flinch a little and swore beneath his breath. "I'm sorry, Lindsay. I didn't mean that the way it sounded—like you did the wrong thing."

She waved his protest aside. "Let's...forget about what I did for now. This is about you and Brittany...and your baby."

He drew in a deep breath and forced out the words he'd never told another soul. "Brittany didn't want to tell anyone about the baby. She didn't want her friends and family to think we were getting married because we 'had' to. And I felt guilty enough—wondering if that was the only reason I was going through with the marriage—that I agreed. So we had the wedding of Brittany's dreams—this lavish affair with the who's who of San Francisco filling the aisles. We went on our honeymoon, and a few weeks later, Brittany told me she'd miscarried."

"Oh, Ryder. I'm so sorry."

"I was already working at her father's firm, and I'd gone to Sacramento for a few days for the grand opening of a mall when she called to give me the news."

Lindsay didn't say the words again but moved close until their hips brushed and reached out to take his hand. The inside of her arm ran alongside the length of his, and she leaned her head against his shoulder. The warmth and compassion of her touch surrounded him, propping him up at a time when he needed it.

"I was devastated—and I thought Brittany was, as well. A year or so into our marriage, I told her I was willing to try again, but she told me she wasn't ready. That the loss was still too fresh. I tried to understand. After all, I couldn't possibly know what she'd gone through. So I waited and waited and waited some more for Brittany to be the one to bring it up. But she never did. She wanted us to keep our focus on our careers, working for her father, attending all the parties, rubbing elbows with the rich and famous.

"But before long, it all seemed so empty to me, so meaningless. We started fighting more and more, and when I told her I wanted to leave Baines and Associates, she told me leaving the company would be the same as leaving her.

"My parents have been happily married for over thirty-five years. Divorce wasn't something I took lightly. I tried to remind her about the plans we'd made when she thought she was having a baby. How we'd move out to the suburbs, find a big house with a huge yard, the perfect place to raise our kids… And that's when Brittany told me she had no intention of ever getting pregnant."

"Ever?" Lindsay echoed, picking up on the wording Brittany had used just as he had.

"Right. No intention of ever getting pregnant. Not of ever getting pregnant *again*, but of ever getting pregnant. Period."

"But she—"

"Lied. About the pregnancy, about the miscarriage, all of it."

"Oh, Ryder."

"I know." His mouth twisted in a grimace. "How could I be so stupid to have fallen for it?"

"You weren't stupid! You believed what Brittany told you."

"You know, the crazy part is that you'd think knowing the baby wasn't real would make it easier to deal with. And yet somehow finding out the truth made me feel like I'd lost that child all over again."

"Because your feelings *were* real. Those plans you talked about—the house, the yard, the kids—that was all real, and Brittany took that from you, not once, but twice." A betrayal still so fresh Lindsay couldn't possibly tell him about Robbie. Not now. Now yet.

"Anyway, I wanted you to understand why I married Brittany, why we got divorced and why I would never, ever go back to her after the way she lied to me."

"I…I understand, Ryder."

"Look, we can go back inside if you want. I know coming back here, showing everyone how much you've changed, means a lot to you. And I don't want anyone to have any doubts about who I want to be with tonight."

Lindsay shook her head as she reached over to touch the side of his face. "I don't care who sees us together. All I care about is us being together."

Pressing her hand against his cheek, he asked, "Come home with me?"

Lindsay nodded and rose, her hand still linked with his. "Yes."

As they walked back to the parking lot, a burst of light and laughter spilled out as the French doors leading from the ballroom to the grounds in back of the house burst open. Lindsay glanced back and thought she caught a brief glimpse of dark hair and a red dress.

She didn't want to believe she and Ryder's ex had anything in common. But like Brittany, she'd let a lie go on for too long. And just like Brittany, Lindsay feared when she told Ryder the truth, she, too, would lose him.

Chapter Fifteen

"Like this?" Robbie asked as he and Ryder knelt along the living room baseboards, carefully running a line of blue tape on the refinished hardwood floors.

Lindsay had finally settled on the pale blue that now decorated the living room walls. The three of them had worked together on the paint job with Lindsay and Robbie focusing on the white space while Ryder concentrated on the more detailed work of cutting in around the windows and doors and along the ceiling. Now only the trim work remained—a glossy white to finish off the room.

"You got it. I think I might have to hire you on full-time," Ryder told the boy and had to hide a smile when Robbie matter-of-factly replied, "I have to finish school first."

"Good idea. That'll make your mom happy, for sure."

With his head bent low over the next section of tape, Robbie said, "Tyler told me him and his dad do stuff together all the time."

"'He' and his dad," Ryder corrected, hearing Lindsay's voice in his head even though he'd teased her more than once about being the 'grammar police.' "And yes, Bryce spends a lot of time with both Tyler and Brayden."

Robbie nodded, but Ryder would bet it wasn't his friends he was thinking about as the tape went a little crooked. He pulled the piece off to start over, and Ryder didn't bother to tell the boy it didn't need to be perfect. Robbie was, after all, his mother's son.

And just as Robbie wouldn't rush to finish the job, neither would he rush to say what was really on his mind. Unlike Ryder's nephews, who said whatever fleeting, more-often-than-not-embarrassing thoughts popped into their heads, Robbie worked his way around a point as if traversing a maze filled with false starts, dead ends and quite a bit of backtracking.

"Yeah, that's what Tyler said. They built a remote-control airplane together. It crashed, though, so he couldn't show me how it works, but he said it went really fast."

"I bought that plane for Tyler as a birthday present." And Ryder was pretty sure Bryce had gotten as big a kick out of it as his son had.

"Yeah, Tyler said you're a really cool uncle. Almost as cool as his dad."

"Only almost, huh?" he joked. Considering how both of Bryce's boys adored their dad, "almost as cool" was high praise. And as little as a few weeks ago, he'd told Lindsay being the cool uncle was enough. Now it wasn't even close to enough. As much as he loved his nephews, they couldn't fill the emptiness inside him. Not the way Lindsay and Robbie could.

His gaze sincere behind his glasses, Robbie vowed, "I think you'd make the greatest dad."

"Thanks, Robbie. I think you'd make the greatest son."

Dropping his focus to the roll of tape in his hand, the boy scraped at the ragged edge. "My dad didn't think so."

Ah, hell. He should have known that's where Robbie was going with the conversation. And while a part of him wished he'd found a way to take a detour around the touchy subject, another part of him wanted answers Lindsay had never given. "Does your mom ever talk about him?"

Robbie shook his head. "Not really," he mumbled. "I used to ask, but—" One shoulder lifted in a halfhearted shrug. "It made her sad. So I stopped."

"You're a good kid, Robbie, to think about your mom's feelings like that."

Ryder could only imagine it hurt Robbie's feelings, too, knowing he had a father out in the world somewhere. A father who'd never bothered to get to know him.

Pirelli's loss, he thought with more than a touch of anger, for missing out on what a great kid he had. And when the boy rested his head against his shoulder, the longing he hadn't let himself feel for such a long, long time settled into his chest, taking up what he feared would be a permanent residence there.

"I saw some letters and pictures of him and my mom that she kept in her drawer."

Ryder swallowed. "Pictures, huh?"

"Yeah, I think they're really old." Robbie gave a small laugh. "She looks funny in them. She's real skinny, and her hair's kinda fuzzy and she's wearing glasses."

Maybe it was natural for Lindsay to hold on to photos of Tony Pirelli. Okay, so he hadn't wanted any mementos from his time with Brittany, taking the bare essentials of his belongings when he'd moved out. He'd wanted to leave everything—the memories, the betrayals, the lies—behind him.

Just because Lindsay wanted to keep a photo or two,

that didn't mean anything. Certainly not that she was still in love with Tony after all these years... Did it?

"I think I know why it made her so sad when I asked about my dad," Robbie confessed, his voice barely above a whisper.

"Why's that, bud?"

Robbie held so still and so silent that Ryder didn't think the boy was going to answer him. Finally, though, his shoulders jerked as he gulped in a big breath of air and exhaled the words in a rush. "I saw another picture, too. One of him in a uniform, and I think—I think my dad's dead."

"Lindsay... We need to talk."

The paintbrush she'd been cleaning with the backyard hose slipped from her hand, clattering against the metal tray. The grim, slightly shocked tone of Ryder's voice registered almost before the words did, and she took a moment to turn off the water before pushing to her feet on shaky legs.

Oh, God. He knows.

This was it. The moment she'd waited for, the moment she'd dreaded. She'd known she was playing with fire, putting off telling Ryder the truth. At some point, something was bound to slip out. What was it? Some casual mention of Robbie's birth date, nine months on from the night she and Ryder had spent together? One of the many similarities she'd noticed between father and son over the past few weeks? Or maybe it was the undeniable bond the two of them had already formed.

"Ryder, I—"

"No, please, let me say this. I don't know—I've tried to be patient. I know coming back here couldn't have been easy for you, and I thought—I'd hoped that if I gave you time, you'd start to open up. To talk to me the way I've always been able to talk to you."

The midday sun was shining brightly in an almost shockingly blue sky, but it was the confusion and uncertainty swirling in Ryder's emerald gaze that had Lindsay closing her eyes. The hurt in his expression sent sharp shards of pain straight to her heart.

"I meant what I said the night of the reunion. You're the only one I ever told about Brittany's lies about the fake pregnancy and miscarriage. I guess I was afraid I'd feel worse, bringing those angry and bitter and painful emotions up all over again. But talking to you, sharing that with you, made me feel better. Like the part of myself that was wounded and festering could finally start to heal. Like we could really move forward because there was nothing in the past—no secrets, no lies—to hold us back."

"Ryder, I am so sorry."

"That's why I have to ask..."

Yes, you're Robbie's father.

"Did you tell Robbie his father's dead?"

"Did I—what?"

"Robbie found some letters from Tony along with old pictures of the two of you and of Tony in his uniform... He told me he thought his dad was dead. I didn't know what to say! I mean, for the poor kid to think— You didn't tell him that, did you, Lindsay?"

"No! Of course not! I never told Robbie his father was dead! I don't know why he would believe that. What—exactly what did he tell you?"

"About the letters and the pictures. About how his questions about his father made you sad and how one day you were crying because an old friend had been killed overseas."

"An old friend..." Lindsay's voice trailed off as a painful memory washed over her. "There was a guy I knew in college when Robbie was still a toddler. He ended up going into the air force. We kept in touch—a few emails here and there, cards at Christmas—and then a few years ago…he was killed in a training exercise. When I heard the news, Robbie asked why I was crying, and I told him an old friend of mine who was in the service had been killed. After seeing that picture of Tony in his uniform, Robbie must have assumed…"

The weight of the burden her son had been carrying crashed down on Lindsay, and she sank onto the bench tucked in amid her grandmother's overgrown asparagus ferns and spider plants. Wrapping her hands around her waist, she leaned forward as if she could keep the pain trapped inside. "I swear, Ryder, I had no idea he thought— All these years, no wonder he never asked any questions about…his father."

Ryder sat beside her and ran a comforting hand down the length of her spine. "I believe you, sweetheart, and I never should have asked. But you know you have to tell him, right? I don't know what happened between you and Tony all those years ago, but the Pirellis are good people. Robbie has a whole family of aunts, uncles and cousins he's never met."

"Oh, Ryder." His caring, his concern, every one of the words he spoke sliced at her heart.

"Do you want me to be there with you when you tell Robbie about Tony—"

"I…I don't need to tell Robbie about Tony."

"You do, Lindsay! Of course you do. He needs to know the truth."

Forcing the words past the ache in her throat, she said, "I don't need to tell him about Tony because Tony isn't his father. You are."

Once, during football practice in college, Ryder had taken a hit hard enough to suffer a concussion. His focus had been straight ahead on a play down the field. The safety had come around the corner and sacked him, driving him to the ground hard enough for his helmet to bounce off the turf.

He'd tried climbing to his feet, but the whole world had tilted beneath him, leaving him dizzy and sick to his stomach...

Lindsay Brookes was half the size of that long-ago defensive player, but she couldn't have hit him any harder.

"Robbie's...mine?"

Her blue-green eyes huge in her pale face, she nodded. "That night we were...together, I ended up pregnant."

"But you and Tony Pirelli—"

"We were friends. *Just* friends. Back then, there was no one else. Only you." Pushing away from the wrought-iron bench, she said, "I am so sorry, Ryder. I was going to tell you—"

Still reeling from the news—Robbie was his?—Ryder shook his head. "When? Right before you left town to go back to Phoenix?"

No wonder she hadn't wanted to talk about the future. He didn't believe she'd ever had any intention of staying in Clearville any more than he could believe she would have told him about Robbie—about his son—if the truth hadn't slipped out.

"No, not like that. I needed time—"

"To do what? Spend the past few weeks lying to me?" While he'd foolishly spent that same time falling in love with her.

"I was going to tell you. That's why I came back."

"That's why you came back now. But what about ten years ago? Why the hell didn't you tell me then?"

"By the time I found out I was pregnant, you were gone! You'd already left for early practice, to go off and fulfill your dream of a college football career before making it in the pros! Everyone at school knew that. The whole town knew that was your plan."

"Plans change, Lindsay!" Finding out Robbie was his son changed...everything. Including how he felt about the boy's mother.

"Yes, and if I had told you, your whole life would have turned upside down and you would have hated me for it."

"Don't tell me how I would have felt. You have no idea how I feel." To know for the second time in his life that a woman he loved had lied to him, betrayed him, manipulated him for *years*... What was it about him that made him such a sucker when it came to falling for a woman's lies?

"Okay, then, let's talk about how I felt, Ryder. Do you have any idea how devastated I felt those last weeks in high school when you would walk by and look right through me? Or how it almost destroyed me when you and Brittany got back together just in time for prom?"

"Prom? You're talking about prom? Is that what this is about? Some kind of revenge?"

"No, it was about me being eighteen years old, heartbroken, pregnant and scared out of my mind! I did what I thought was best at the time."

"At the time, but what about later, Lindsay? Why didn't you tell me then?"

"When?" she cried. "When I heard you and Brittany had moved in together? When I learned you'd gotten engaged? When you were married and working for her family? What would have been the best time for me to give you a call out of the blue and tell you Robbie was your son?"

Her words hammered into Ryder, but his anger deflected the truth behind them. "You should have told me. All these years—" *I should have known.*

"Mom?" Robbie's voice drifted out from inside the house. "Are you guys done out there? I thought we were going for a burger in town."

The boy slipped through the screen door, letting it slam shut behind him, and Ryder couldn't help noticing Lindsay flinch at the sound. She'd wrapped her arms around her waist, an effort to hold herself together or maybe to keep from grabbing Robbie away from him.

Robbie. His son, who stood right outside arm's reach. "Robbie—"

"What's going on?"

Lindsay had told Ryder how smart Robbie was, and Ryder had seen that side of Lindsay in the boy as he'd focused on whatever Ryder had been willing to teach him. Robbie was far too observant and far too sensitive not to realize something was wrong.

"Your mom and I were just talking."

His eyes—eyes that Ryder had thought were his mother's but could now see were more green than blue—were wide behind the wire frames of his glasses. "It sounded like you were fighting."

"Not fighting, but we were having a…discussion, and we may have raised our voices. That happens sometimes when grown-ups feel strongly about something."

"But…but you never yell." Bewilderment filled Robbie's voice as he looked at his mother. "You always say the louder you talk, the less the other person is going to listen."

That sounded like something Lindsay would say, and Ryder didn't doubt she practiced what she preached. Hadn't he noticed how she kept her emotions tightly wrapped beneath that polite, professional shell? Hadn't he taken a bit of pleasure from getting a rise out of her by tweaking her anger when she first came to town? And then more recently—had it only been two days ago—losing himself in an overwhelming satisfaction as passion shattered that coolly polite image and she came apart in his arms?

"And Ryder's a really great guy," Robbie was saying, "so why would you yell at him?"

"Robbie—"

The boy didn't let Lindsay finish. His hesitant glance flicked toward Ryder and away again. "Tyler said he heard his mom and dad talking. He said that you and Ryder are, like, dating. And Tyler says if you like each other enough and date long enough, you'll get married. If you get married, Ryder'll be my dad, and…and I'd really like it if Ryder was my dad."

"Oh, Robbie." Lindsay didn't think it was possible for her heart to break any further and still keep pumping blood through her body. The pain alone should have killed her already. "Sweetheart…come here."

His shoulders slumping, Robbie reluctantly walked over to his mother. Head down, he dug the toe of his sneaker into the grass at his feet. "You and Ryder aren't gonna get married, are you?"

Lindsay didn't dare look over at Ryder in that moment, having already seen anger, shock and betrayal lay waste to any other feelings he might have had for her. "No, sweetie, we aren't getting married. But we do have something to tell you."

It wasn't the way she wanted to do this. To tell Robbie about Ryder when all of their emotions were running so high. When her world was once again spinning out of control. But she didn't have a choice. If she didn't tell Robbie— well, she could practically feel the words building up inside Ryder, sense him trembling to hold them back. It was only a matter of time before he blew, and right time or not, Lindsay wanted to be the one to tell Robbie the truth. He was still her son, too, and she knew him much better and for far longer than Ryder—even if her son did already think he'd make an awesome dad.

"I want to talk to you about your father, Robbie. Ryder told me that you thought your dad was dead."

Her son's gaze instantly cut to Ryder—a hint of hurt

in his expression that Ryder had broken the guy code of silence. "I told him, but— Wait... Do you mean he's not dead?"

"No, Robbie. He's not. Those pictures and letters you found, they were from a boy I knew a long time ago before you were born. And back then, a lot of people thought he was your dad, but he isn't."

His eyebrows gathered in a frown above the wire frames of his glasses. "Then who is my dad?"

"Ryder is, sweetie." Lindsay hadn't known how her son would react when she told him the truth, but the tears filling his eyes were the last thing she'd expected.

"You're my dad?" Accusation cut through the words as he stared at Ryder. "I thought—I thought we were friends!"

Ryder took a small step back as if staggered by the emotional blow before rallying on a deep breath. Kneeling down in front of Robbie, he placed his hands on the boy's shoulders. "We are friends, Robbie. Isn't it possible for us to be friends and for me to be your father, too?"

"But why didn't you tell me before?" her son asked, his words a painful echo of Ryder's. "Why haven't you been my dad all along?"

"Because he didn't know." Robbie's head swung back in her direction as she spoke. "By the time I knew I was pregnant with you, Ryder had already left for college. He'd had a dream of playing football since he was your age, and I was worried that if I told him about you, he'd have to give up that dream. And I didn't want that to happen."

"Football's nothing but a dumb game."

"Robbie—"

"You're right, Robbie," Ryder said. "It is only a game, and there's nothing...nothing more important to me than being your dad. I know this is all a lot to think about, but all I'm asking for is the chance to prove that to you."

Ducking his head to rub a fist beneath his glasses, the boy mumbled, "Can I go to my room now?"

"Sure, sweetie, go ahead." Lindsay could see Ryder wanted to argue as his hands reluctantly slid from Robbie's shoulders, but her son was already at an age where he was embarrassed by his emotions. So even though she ached to pull him into his arms, cradle him on her lap and kiss all his hurts away as she had done when he was three, she let him go instead.

Ryder stayed in his crouched position, one knee sinking into the soft grass, his forearms braced against a powerful denim-clad thigh for a long time once Robbie disappeared inside.

"He needs time, Ryder," she said softly as he stared after their son.

Emerald-tipped daggers shot straight to her heart with the dark look he gave her. "He wouldn't if you'd told us both the truth from the beginning."

"That's easy to say now, but—"

"Easy!" He spat the word at her as he jumped to his feet. "You think any of this is easy!"

"No! Look, whether you believe it or not, I'm glad you want to be a father to Robbie. But you're saying that as a grown man to a ten-year-old boy. You're not thinking about what it would have been like back then—as a teenage father to a newborn infant. You have no idea how terrifying it was—"

Her voice broke as she remembered those early days when Robbie had been so little, so helpless. When she'd been so scared to pick him up and at the same time afraid to put him down. When every sound from the tiniest squawk to the loudest cry had sent panic rushing through her and she'd been sure she was doing everything wrong...

Through it all, she held on to one simple fact. "I did what I thought was the best thing to do at the time."

But if she was looking to Ryder for sympathy or un-derstanding, she would have been sorely disappointed. If anything, his expression turned stone-cold. He'd judged her, found her guilty, and nothing she could say or do from now on would change his mind. Holding on to her compo-sure like a lifeline, she turned and walked away.

And like her son, the last thing Lindsay wanted was for Ryder Kincaid to see her cry.

Chapter Sixteen

Lindsay was still staring out the front window at the empty driveway when her grandmother took her by the arm and led her away. "They've only been gone an hour. Watching won't bring Robbie back any faster."

"I know, but—"

"No buts. Robbie's spent plenty of time with Bryce's boys over the past few weeks."

"That was before."

Before she'd told Ryder and Robbie they were father and son. Before Ryder made the announcement to his parents and siblings. Before the Kincaids wanted to have a party welcoming Robbie to the family—a party Lindsay had opted not to attend.

"Before" was only three days ago, but it already felt like a lifetime.

Especially when Robbie was barely talking to her and Ryder had retreated so far behind a polite mask she no longer recognized him. They'd made the decision to keep their emotions out of the situation, to put Robbie first and not allow their own feelings to come into play. But her son was nothing if not observant, and she knew he wasn't fooled.

"Yes, and this is now, and now we are going to stay busy."

"I don't think anything's going to keep my mind off Robbie." *Or off Ryder...*

"Come on, I need your help rehanging the pictures in the living room now that the painting is all done." They'd taken the family portraits down a few days before, carefully stacking them on the dining room table.

"I should have paid more attention as we were taking them down," Ellie was saying. "I like them to be in chronological order, and sometimes I can't remember..."

Standing on a stepladder, Lindsay hung a picture of her grandparents on their wedding day. "You two look so happy," she said with a wistful smile as she carefully straightened the frame.

"We were young. We didn't know any better."

"Gran! You adored Grandpa. I don't know how many times you told me he was the love of your life."

"And he was, but that didn't mean life was easy. There are always challenges, ups and downs along the way. Love doesn't smooth out the road. But it does make it easier to have someone at your side to share the burdens—and the joys—on that journey."

Ellie handed her another picture. This one of an infant boy. Not the old-fashioned, slightly faded picture of Lindsay's father, but the round-faced, sleepy-eyed baby photo of her son. Startled, Lindsay glanced down into her grandmother's gently aged face and knowing eyes.

How different would life have been with Ryder on that road beside her? Through the long, scary yet exciting months of her pregnancy? Through all of Robbie's milestones—from first tooth, to first word, to first step?

And how devastating to face knowing she'd robbed Ryder of that chance. Robbed *all* of them of that chance.

If she could go back— Lindsay sank down on the step-ladder. She couldn't change the past or give any of them back what they'd lost. All she could do was take that first step toward the future. A future she and Ryder would walk together—if not as a couple, then at least as parents.

"I'm taking the job at the Chamber of Commerce," she announced.

"Oh, Lindsay! I didn't realize you'd made up your mind."

"Ryder and Robbie deserve the chance to have a real relationship."

She would die a little inside, she knew, every time Ryder looked at her with that icy fury in his green eyes. It would be high school all over again, with her loving him from afar and knowing she had no chance… She still didn't know if the decision she had made ten years ago had been one of a selfless mother doing the right thing for her child or that of a selfish girl doing what was best for her.

But this decision she knew without a doubt would be what was best for her son and his father.

Ryder hadn't taken his eye off Robbie since they arrived at Bryce's house. He kept looking for similarities between himself and the boy. Was there something in their slightly crooked smiles? In the shape of their faces? The cowlick they both had on the right side of their forehead?

One minute, he didn't know if he was imagining match-ing traits that weren't there, while in the next, he wondered how he could have been so blind not to have noticed them all along.

One thing he knew for sure, though, was that Robbie was his son. Lindsay wouldn't have told him if it wasn't the truth. Given half a chance, he was sure she wouldn't have told him at all.

Sitting on the back porch steps, he glanced over his shoulder as the screen door squeaked behind him. His mother stepped outside, and her gaze immediately locked on Robbie, as well. But unlike Ryder, she was smiling as she watched the boy play a game of keep-away with his nephews and their dog.

"Lindsay called a few minutes ago," she said as she lowered herself to sit on the porch step beside him.

Ryder wouldn't have thought his already-knotted muscles could get any tighter, but the mention of her name was enough to have his knuckles whitening around the glass of iced tea in his hand. "What did she want?"

"She said Robbie could spend the weekend with you if he wanted."

"The whole weekend, huh?"

His mother's gaze was filled with reproach at the bitter bite of his words. "She's trying, Ryder."

"Like two days will make up for almost ten years." Not to mention she was still planning to go back to Phoenix in two weeks. He'd just found Robbie and soon over a thousand miles would separate them. What kind of relationship could he have with his son over that kind of distance? When would they see each other? A few weeks in the summer and every other Christmas?

"Nothing Lindsay does now can change what happened in the past, and that is something you're both going to have to accept."

"She should have told me," Ryder insisted.

"Yes, that is true. But what would have happened if she had? You were so sure you and Brittany belonged together, so determined to go off to college with her even though your father and I worried about you attending such a big school. You had your whole life planned out from, well, from the time you and Brittany met, it seemed. Lindsay and Robbie were never part of that plan, Ryder."

"You don't think my plans would have changed if I'd known I had a son? You don't think I would have made the right decision?"

"I think at eighteen that would have been a very difficult choice for you to make, and I think that's why Lindsay made it for you."

"You have no idea how terrifying it was."

Lindsay's words, the crack in her voice, the tears she'd tried so hard to hide scraped across his memory. Even after everything she'd done—after the lies, after the betrayal—a part of him had wanted nothing more than to take her into his arms, to hold her against his chest and tell her it would be all right. That they would *all* be all right.

But then he'd thought of Brittany and how broken up she'd been, how *devastated* after her supposed miscarriage, and he refused to let another woman manipulate him.

"I don't know if I can ever forgive her." Saying the words, Ryder felt agonizing claws rip at his guts. After what Lindsay had done, he had every right to hate her. So why did the idea of losing what they had—what he *thought* they'd had—tear him apart inside?

"I can't tell you how to feel," his mother said softly. "But I can tell you one thing. You have an amazing son, and like it or not, you have Lindsay to thank for that. Don't let the pain of the past ruin your joy in the here and now."

His mother squeezed his shoulder in a comforting gesture before pushing away from the porch steps and walking back across the lawn to join the rest of the party. The spot was only empty for a moment or two before his sister came and joined him.

"What are you doing over here by yourself?"

"Finding my joy in the now," he said dryly.

"Yeah? How's that working out for you?" Sydney asked

as she tucked her legs up against her chest and wrapped her arms around her knees.

Ryder shrugged in response as the two of them sat in silence.

"They look so happy, don't they?" she said finally.

Ryder followed his sister's gaze over to where Bryce and Nina stood together. Bryce stood behind his pregnant wife, his hands folded over her still-flat belly. "Yeah, they do."

"At least one of us got it right," she said, a soft thread of wistfulness weaving through the words.

Ryder glanced over in time to see Sydney blinking back tears. "Hey, what's wrong?"

"It's…nothing. You have enough troubles of your own to worry about."

"Actually I'm pretty sick of worrying about my own problems. Maybe listening to yours will help take my mind off them."

"Oh, well, in that case, I'm glad my disaster of a love life will provide you with a convenient distraction."

"That bad, huh? I thought you and Evan we're getting serious."

"So did I."

"What went wrong?"

Tilting her head back, Sydney stared up at the darkening sky. "That's the thing—I don't know. I thought everything was great, that our relationship was going to be the start of something that was going to last. And the next thing I know—wham! Evan says things aren't working, and he wants to take a break. That's what my coming here was supposed to be. A break. Instead I got a call from a friend who lives down the street. She saw a moving truck parked outside our town house. She wanted to make sure we weren't being robbed while I was out of town. No such luck. It was just Evan…moving out."

"Ah, hell, Syd…"

"Can you believe that? He was going to let me walk into our house and find his stuff already gone. Like what we had together didn't mean a thing. Done. Over. And not a damn thing to show for it."

"I'm sorry."

"Yeah," she sniffed. "Me, too."

"Hey, enough of that! Forget about him. He's not worth your time let alone your tears."

"I know but…I loved him, Ry. I really thought he was the one."

The youngest of the Kincaid children, Sydney took after their mother's side of the family with her petite frame and barely five-foot height. Add in the long curly hair and the dusting of freckles across her nose, and she'd always looked younger than her age. And no matter how old she was, Sydney would always be the little sister he and Bryce looked out for. As she furtively brushed a tear from her cheek, those protective instincts roared to life, and Ryder swore beneath his breath. "The guy's a total ass, Syd. To walk out like that without so much as an explanation…"

"Do you have any idea how devastated I felt those last weeks in high school when you would walk by and look right through me?"

"Ryder?"

Sucking in a deep breath, he said, "I'm sorry. About Evan and everything. You didn't deserve to be treated like that. You deserve a guy who's smart enough to realize how lucky he is to have you. Someone who'll hold on and won't let go."

"Thank you for that…although I'm not sure you're still talking about me and Evan."

"There's a part of me that wants to head straight for Seattle and punch Evan right in the face for walking out on you. And then there's a part of me that wants to kick myself in the ass for having done the same damn thing to Lindsay."

"You were a kid, Ryder," Sydney protested, sticking up for him as strongly as he had for her.

"So was Lindsay. And she was pregnant."

"She should have told you," Sydney maintained stubbornly.

"Or maybe I should have asked," Ryder pointed out.

"You couldn't have known."

"I knew we slept together. And I knew Lindsay had gotten pregnant." Ryder had left already that summer to attend practices with other freshmen hoping to make the football team by the time the news of Lindsay's pregnancy was tearing up the Clearville grapevine. Dread had clutched his gut every time the phone rang for the next several weeks as he waited for Lindsay to call and tell him he was the one responsible.

Rapid-fire denial had shot through his head every time.

Couldn't be mine.

It was just one time.

We used protection.

No way. There's no way...

Despite all that, he had waited for a call that never came. And he had been...relieved. He could go on with his life, with the plans he and Brittany had made and focused on for years. He didn't have to think about prenatal exams or Lamaze classes or what it would be like to be responsible for a helpless baby. Midnight feedings, messy diapers, nonstop crying during colic or teething or illness... He hadn't had to deal with any of that.

He hadn't *wanted* to deal with it.

And if Lindsey had told him all those years ago... Ryder wondered if his mother was right. Maybe Lindsay had made the hard choice so he didn't have to.

* * *

Ryder wasn't sure when he first realized something was wrong. He'd been so lost in his own thoughts, he barely remembered saying good-night to Bryce and Nina. His sister-in-law had handed him a paper bag with a borrowed pair of pajamas and an extra toothbrush. The sympathy in her gaze when he confessed he hadn't even considered what the boy might need nearly did him in. Instead he'd gruffly thanked her before he and Robbie headed home.

Home.

Stepping inside the house, he had to admit the word didn't ring true. Wasn't that partly why he spent so much time over at Bryce and Nina's? Because their sprawling, slightly cluttered, slightly chaotic ranch had all the warmth and welcome of a home while his rental had only the cold practicality of convenience? A place to store his stuff and hit the hay at the end of a long day?

He'd shown his son the guest bedroom, where Robbie had changed into his borrowed pajamas, before they settled down on the couch. Robbie found a cartoon playing on a kids' channel Ryder hadn't even known was part of his cable package. Before long, his eyes were drifting shut behind his glasses, but Ryder's suggestion of bedtime was met with a quiet protest.

"Not yet. It's getting to the good part."

One good part led to another even as the boy was yawning enough to make Ryder tired. As the credits started to roll, Ryder said, "Okay, kid. Time for bed."

Robbie dragged his feet down the hall, a sign Ryder contributed to a kid's normal resistance to going to bed combined with being overly tired. But when Robbie stopped short in the bedroom doorway, his gaze locked on the large bed taking up the majority of the almost-empty room, he whispered, "I don't want to stay here."

"Robbie—"

The boy lifted sad, watery eyes to meet Ryder's gaze. "I...I always wanted a dad, and I'm glad, you know, that it's you."

Dropping down to his son's level, Ryder rested his hands on the boy's narrow shoulders. "I'm glad, too, Robbie. For a long time now I've wanted a son, and I couldn't have picked a better kid."

Maybe his mother was right. Maybe he did need to focus more on the good in the present and try to forget the anger and bitterness whenever he thought of the past he couldn't change.

Robbie ducked his head, retreating back into the shy boy Ryder had first met, as he softly repeated, "I always wanted a dad, but I've always had a mom." His skinny chest rose and fell as he tried to swallow the emotion too big for a little boy to hold inside. "I didn't know having both would mean having to choose."

"To choose?" Ryder didn't know what the words meant until Robbie lifted his miserable gaze to meet his.

"I wanna— I want to go home."

Ryder's heart seized in his chest. Fighting Lindsay was one thing, but fighting his own son to keep him in Clearville if it wasn't where he wanted to be was something else. "Back to Phoenix?"

Robbie shook his head. "No, back to Grandma Ellie's house. I want my mom."

"I'm sorry about this," Ryder said to Lindsay as he stood in the entryway of the quiet house staring at the stairwell leading to the bedrooms upstairs. His son had disappeared up those stairs almost as soon as they arrived. He'd given Lindsay a quick hug and then left Ryder behind without a backward glance. "I didn't want to wake you—"

The words scraped against his throat, but he wasn't surprised. Failure had ripped away every protective inch of skin, leaving him raw and bleeding. One night. He couldn't prove to Robbie—or Lindsay—that he could be a good father for even so much as one night.

"I wasn't sleeping," Lindsay admitted.

The sconces he'd rewired worked perfectly, and Lindsay had turned them on the lowest setting. But even that faint glow illuminated her pale features and the truth to her words. She hadn't been sleeping, probably not for the past few days, judging by the bruised look around her blue-green eyes.

How many sleepless nights had there been over the past nine years? Nights spent worrying at Robbie's side through teething and colds and stomach flu? Nights in her own bed, tossing and turning with her thoughts consumed by less easily defined concerns—finding the right schools, the right classes, the right friends?

"He had a good time over at Bryce's. I want you to know that. He was playing with Tyler and Brayden and chasing Cowboy all over the yard."

"I know. He told me when I called over there."

"I think—when you asked him if he wanted to spend the weekend with me—that he thought we'd spend that whole time over at my brother's." And why wouldn't Robbie have wanted that? Hadn't Ryder already figured out his brother and sister-in-law were the perfect parents, the perfect family, while he— Hell, he didn't have a clue what he was doing. "Once he got to my place and realized it was just the two of us, it was a different story."

Robbie had said he hadn't wanted to choose between his mother and newfound father, but the boy had made his preference known when he asked to go back to Lindsay.

"He's been through a lot the past few days, Ryder. Give him a little time."

Time. That was what Lindsay had asked for when she first told him about Robbie, and he'd thrown the idea back in her face. All he'd thought about was the time he'd already missed. He hadn't thought about the time Robbie would need to adjust to such a big change. "This is my fault. I shouldn't have pushed—"

"It's no one's fault, Ryder."

Pacing back and forth, Ryder went on as if Lindsay hadn't spoken. "I don't even have a room for him at my place. I mean, I have a guest room, but it's not a little boy's room. I don't have any of his stuff. Toys or games—hell, I don't even know what toys and games he likes to play with."

Lindsay stopped him on his tenth pass around the room. Stepping in front of him, she caught his shoulders and held him still. "You'll figure it out."

"How can you be so sure?"

"Because I know how you feel. I know what a big surprise this has been."

"How did you do it? How did you handle finding out you were going to have a baby?"

"Well, first I panicked." The slightest hint of a smile teased her lips, and it was all Ryder could do not to pull her into his arms, claim her mouth with his—

But he wouldn't. He *couldn't*. Too much was at stake with Robbie caught between them for Ryder to risk taking that kind of chance with Lindsay. Their relationship as parents was the only one that could matter now. Stomping out the relentless ache of desire, he forced himself to focus on the sound coming from Lindsay's lips rather than on the tempting shape, texture and taste...

"Panicked, huh? Good to know I've got that one down already."

"After the panic faded, I felt this sense of amazement that I was going to be a mother and give birth to this child who was a part of me. A part of *us*. And I still feel that way now. Some days it's harder than others to find that wonder now that Robbie's no longer this perfectly tiny infant, but it's still there. That love and joy never goes away even when times are tough and I question if I'm doing the right thing."

She ducked her head quickly, but not before he saw the tears shimmering in her eyes. They were still there a second later when she shook her hair back and met his gaze. "That's all I ever tried to do. To make the best choice for Robbie…for our son. And that's why I've decided to move back to Clearville."

Chapter Seventeen

With her decision made, Lindsay moved quickly. Her first call was to her parents, who were understandably surprised by what they saw as a sudden decision, but once she explained the whole story—including the news that Ryder was Robbie's father—they both said they understood. As teachers they would have several opportunities throughout the year to come to Clearville and visit, and Lindsay had the feeling her parents would be looking to their hometown as a place to retire just as Ellie had hoped.

Her second call was to give notice at her job. Her new boss had said all the right things, but Lindsay had the feeling he had her position filled by the time they hung up the phone. She might have been more upset about being so easily replaced if she hadn't had another call to make—one to Patricia Bennett, who was thrilled that Lindsay was taking the position at the Chamber of Commerce.

She'd talked to Robbie, who, despite Ryder's concern, was eager to make his stay in Clearville a permanent one—once he realized Lindsay was staying as well and he didn't have to choose between his mother and his new dad. He'd even adjusted to the point where he split his time between Ellie's house and Ryder's when Lindsay went back to Phoenix to oversee the packing and move, though most of their furniture would be going into storage.

They were staying with Ellie until their condo in Phoenix sold and Lindsay found a new place in Clearville. Her grandmother had made it clear they could stay as long as they liked, and Lindsay had to admit, she was in no real hurry to move out. Robbie had been through so many changes lately...

The buzz at the front door was one of those changes. When Ryder was working at the house, she'd gotten used to him walking in after a quick knock. Now she had to get used to listening for the sound of the bell.

She sucked in a deep breath, emotionally preparing for the pain of seeing him again. It would get easier with time. It had to. A person couldn't live with a broken and bleeding heart forever, and hers ached every time Ryder stopped by. The heat of his anger had faded, but what was left behind was a cold, remote shell of the man she'd known these past few weeks.

No more teasing smiles, no more subtle flirting, no more intimate glances... He seemed determined to keep an emotional distance, while Lindsay longed for nothing more than the feel of his arms around her, holding her tight as if he never wanted to let her go.

But she couldn't change the past any more than she could change how much she loved Ryder, and somehow she would have to learn to live with both.

"Robbie," she called as she headed for the entryway. "Do you have your stuff ready to go? Ryder's here early."

Her son's "in a minute" drifted down the stairs as she

opened the door, but the man on the other side wasn't Ryder. It was possibly the last man she ever thought she'd see.

"Tony? Oh, my God, Tony! What are you doing here?"

Ten years might have passed, but she would have recognized Tony Pirelli anywhere. He was quite a bit bigger and, she'd be willing to bet, quite a bit badder, but still so much the same as the boy she remembered. Same dark hair, same dark eyes, same attitude...

Wearing a pair of faded-to-ash jeans and a black T-shirt stretched across his wide shoulders, he braced a hand casually against the doorjamb as if showing up out of the blue after a decade was no big deal. "Theresa called. She told me the big secret's out, and it's all over town that Ryder Kincaid is Robbie's father. I figured you could probably use a friend."

"I can't believe you're here." Seeing Tony immediately swept Lindsay back to the long, lazy days of summer and the friendship that had formed between two loners on the outside looking in. "It is so good to see you again!"

He shrugged as he followed her inside the living room. "My cousin Sophia had a baby last year, my sister's engaged to some cowboy and I'm the only one in the family who hasn't seen the kid or met the fiancé, so I thought what the hell?"

Lindsay didn't think the motive for his arrival was anything so simple. "Is your family glad now that they know the truth?"

Having seen the way Ryder's parents had welcomed Robbie as their new grandson, she could only imagine how hard it had been for Tony's family to have thought they were missing out on Robbie's life all these years.

"Naw, they're still pissed."

"Why?"

"They're mad that I 'let' them believe the worst for so

long." He rolled his eyes as he leaned back against the cushions. "As if anything else was an option."

"We both knew what everyone would think, what they would assume."

"And the plan worked. No one knew Ryder Kincaid was Robbie's father. Hell, I never even knew."

"You never asked."

"If you'd wanted me to know, you would have told me."

"You never suspected?"

"That it was Kincaid? No way. When you said you were pregnant and couldn't tell the father, I thought the guy was probably married."

"Tony!"

"What was I supposed to think? I sure never would have guessed you had a thing for the golden-boy jock."

"He was more than a jock."

"If you say so."

"Hey, Mom, I can't find my tennis shoes—" Robbie's clattering footsteps came to a sudden stop in the living room doorway as he caught sight of Tony sitting on the couch.

Pushing to her feet, she said, "We left them on the back porch, remember? After you came back covered in mud when Ryder took you and Tyler fishing."

"Oh. Yeah."

"Come over here for a second." She placed a hand on his shoulder as he came to stand at her side. "This is Tony Pirelli."

"I know. I recognize him from his picture." Robbie's eyes narrowed as he gazed at the man. "I thought you were my dad."

"Yeah, I know." Tony stood and stuffed his hands in his back pockets. Lindsay couldn't imagine the dangers he'd faced over the years, first in the marines and even now in his job as a bodyguard. But she also couldn't picture the tough guy looking any more uncomfortable as he eyed her son.

"I thought you were dead."

Tony rocked back on his heels and shot a glance at Lindsay. "That I did not know."

"It's…a long story."

"Why is he here?"

"Robbie, don't be rude. Tony's a friend, and he came to see me."

"I thought Ryder was your friend."

Prickles of heat flared across her cheekbones. Had she imagined the slight emphasis Robbie had placed on that last word? She had, after all, always referred to his father as an old friend. She'd talked to her son about the birds and bees in general terms, but she really didn't want him to be thinking about the subject as it related to her sex life.

"He is, but I can have more than one friend."

"I don't think that's right," he muttered beneath his breath.

"Well, you don't get to decide. Now go get your stuff ready for going to Ryder's."

Lindsay watched pointedly until her son turned and trudged up the stairs, a full three-count between each footfall. She didn't need to look to know Tony was already smirking.

"I can't figure out who he's trying to protect—you or Kincaid."

"It's been hard on him. On both of them."

"But not on you?"

"I'm not the one who had to learn the truth."

"No, you're the one who had to keep the secret. Kincaid had some big football scholarship back then, didn't he?"

Tony might have been only a visitor, but Ryder had been big news that last summer. "He did."

"Uh-huh."

A heavy weight of blame landed in those two syllables, and Lindsay's back went up instinctively, feeling the need to defend Ryder even though Tony was only trying to defend *her*. "How would you feel if a woman showed up and told you that you were a father?"

He crossed his arms as he shook his head. "Not going to happen."

"Well, it did to Ryder, so give him a break."

Her friend's knowing gaze saw too much. "You fell for him again, didn't you, Lindsay? After all these years… Or maybe it's more like you're *still* in love with him after all these years. So I guess the only question is, are you going to tell him this time?"

Ryder was in the grocery store when he first heard the rumors of Tony Pirelli's return.

He was still somewhat amazed by how much food a skinny nine-year-old could pack away. Eating out every night wasn't the healthiest choice, and he couldn't expect Bryce and Nina or his parents to keep feeding them.

A fully stocked refrigerator wasn't the only change to his bachelor pad over the past few weeks. He'd cleared out the cold, impersonal guest room and transformed it into a boy's bedroom complete with a twin bed, a matching dresser and bookshelf and a few action-movie posters on the walls.

His mother and Nina had both offered to lend a hand with the redecorating, but the job had been one Ryder wanted to do on his own. Or so he told himself until he walked into the department store at the mall and realized how completely out of his element he was. As lost as Lindsay must have felt the day they went shopping at the flooring warehouse, and he'd realized what he really wanted was to have her at his side.

And not just for shopping but for all the moments he

and Robbie spent together as father and son. For all the long days and nights he spent alone, missing her smile, her sweetness, her warmth. Missing *her*.

And yet those brief times when they were together, when he stopped by Ellie's to pick Robbie up or when Lindsay dropped him off, those moments were pure hell. Like staring into the sun, it hurt to look at her. He ached to pull her into his arms, to taste the sweetness of her kiss, to hear her laugh. But even though they'd gotten past the tense, awkward silences, even though Lindsay smiled at him every so often, the distance between them remained. A polite, platonic distance that was slowly killing him.

Deal with it, Ryder reminded himself harshly. He'd already lived through a failed marriage and a divorce. He'd blown his friendship with Lindsay, not once, but twice, and couldn't count on the third time being the charm. Not when every move he made affected Robbie. He was a father now. He had to be responsible. To sacrifice the way Lindsay had all those years ago and again with moving back to Clearville, all for the good of their child.

So even though he longed to call her and ask if Robbie liked watermelon, if he should try to get the boy to eat more vegetables, if Robbie really was allowed to eat a bowl of ice cream before bed every night as he said—to ask any damn question he could think of simply to hear the sound of her voice—Ryder left his cell phone in his back pocket and wheeled the cart over to the produce section.

He was debating how to choose between two mini watermelons when not-so-hushed whispers drifted over from the next aisle. One of the female voices sounded like Cherrie Macintosh's, but that wouldn't have been enough to grab his attention. The mention of Lindsay's name, though, had him freezing with the fruit in his hand.

"She's telling everyone Ryder Kincaid's the boy's father, but if that's true, then why would *he* come back?"

Ryder couldn't make out the other woman's question, but Cherrie's response came through loud and clear. "Tall, dark and dangerous as ever!"

He could think of only one man in Lindsay's life who matched that description. But what the hell was Tony Pirelli doing back in Clearville?

As much as Ryder wanted to ask Lindsay that question, he didn't get the chance. When he went to pick up Robbie, Ellie informed him that Lindsay had left to go to a Chamber of Commerce board meeting. Robbie, however, was quick to fill Ryder in on Tony's visit as they drove toward the movie theater in town.

"Mom said he's come back because his sister lives here now and she's getting married and stuff." Robbie's disgruntled tone made it plain what he thought of that explanation. "I don't like him."

Ryder supposed it was another sign of his inexperience as a parent that his first instinct was to high-five his son rather than give some kind of "let's all try to get along" speech. "Did she say how long he's going to be in town?"

"Uh-uh. He didn't stay very long, but she said she'd see him later before he left."

"You weren't eavesdropping, were you, Robbie?"

"Maybe." The boy slanted him a sideways glance. "Will you tell my mom?"

"I think this time we'll keep it between the two of us."

"So, what are you gonna do about my mom and Tony?"

The question was one Ryder still didn't have an answer to two hours later when they left the movie theater. Logically he knew there was nothing he could do about it. Lindsay had every right to have as many guy friends as she wanted. Hell, she had just as much of a right to have as many *boy*friends as she wanted. She was a smart, sexy, single woman.

But logic alone couldn't keep Ryder from wanting to track down Tony Pirelli and to tell the other man the town of Clearville wasn't big enough for both of them. He wanted everyone to know without a doubt that Robbie was his son…that Lindsay was his woman. It was a kind of old-fashioned, masochistic thinking that was likely to get his ass kicked and not necessarily by Tony.

You have to do the right thing for Robbie.

But why did staying away from Lindsay feel so wrong?

Robbie stopped short on the sidewalk outside the movie theater, and Ryder braced a hand on his son's back. "Whoa there, bud. What's wrong?"

"Look," his son whispered, "it's him."

Ryder didn't need to ask who *he* was. He didn't remember much about Tony Pirelli from ten years ago, but the man looked enough like his cousins, Nick and Drew, for Ryder to immediately recognize Tony as he stepped out from an antiques store down the street.

The Hope Chest wasn't exactly the place Ryder would expect the dark-haired, scruffy, rough-around-the-edges guy to shop, but then he remembered that Tony's cousin Sophia was the manager there.

"Robbie, why don't you run into the bakery and see what cookies Debbie made today?"

"We already had popcorn at the movie."

Strike two as a parent—distracting his kid with junk food—but Ryder handed his son a twenty and said, "We'll save them for after dinner. And brush our teeth twice. Now go on."

"But, Dad…" Robbie ducked his head as his voice trailed off on that one small word. A word Ryder hadn't realized how badly he wanted to hear coming from his son's lips until the moment it sank into his soul, warming his heart with the love he'd already felt.

Because even before he'd found out Robbie was his,

the boy had been a part of Lindsay—a part of the woman Ryder loved.

"Go on," he repeated around the lump in his throat. "It's going to be okay. Everything's going to be okay."

Robbie took the money with a sigh, and Ryder watched as his son slipped through the bakery's door before turning his attention back to Tony Pirelli. It wasn't a gunfight at high noon, but meeting face-to-face on Main Street still had the feeling of a showdown.

"Pirelli, I heard you were back in town."

"Good news travels fast," the dark-haired man drawled. "'Course it took ten years for you to figure out Robbie's your kid."

With Pirelli's military background and training, he'd lay Ryder flat in a second, but that didn't stop him from getting in the other man's face. "Robbie is the best thing that ever happened to me!"

"Yeah?" Tony challenged. "You tell Lindsay that yet?"

Some of Ryder's fury waned at the point-blank question. He hadn't told Lindsay how fortunate he felt to have Robbie in his life…to have her in his life. But he wasn't about to admit any of that to Tony. "What happens between Lindsay and me is none of your business."

The other man crossed his arms over his chest. "I'll take that as a no. You know, I was here ten years ago to pick up the pieces you left behind when you broke her heart. Hurt her again, and it'll be pieces of you that will need to be put back together. Most people don't get a second chance. By my count, you're on your third. Don't blow it this time."

"Your first day of work," Patricia greeted Lindsay with a huge smile as she stepped into the Chamber of Commerce office. "Isn't this exciting?"

Lindsay wished she could dial up a bit more enthusiasm about her new job, but like most of her days recently, she felt as if she was simply going through the motions. Putting one foot in front of the other and reminding herself that life would get better. That the pain in her heart would fade, that every time she saw Ryder wouldn't make it break all over again.

It didn't help that Robbie had spent the past weekend at Ryder's place, leaving Lindsay with little else to do but miss him. Miss them both.

Trying to summon up some enthusiasm, she returned Patricia's smile as she said, "I've been looking forward to getting started. I've had some more ideas for promoting the benefit rodeo and—"

"And I would love to hear them all," Patricia said as she circled the desk, "but this morning, we have a special meeting to go to." Before Lindsay even had the chance to set her purse down, Patricia took her by the elbow and guided her back down the hallway and out the office door. "There's a man in town who has a major project in the works, and he wants to tell you about his idea for building a new future in Clearville."

"I haven't heard about a new project." Granted, she'd only been at her job for all of five minutes, but wouldn't she have heard through the grapevine if something big was happening in town?

"Oh, don't worry. He'll tell you all about it."

"Shouldn't I know something about the project before the meeting?" Lindsay asked, a touch of panic building inside her as she struggled to keep up with the quick pace Patricia had set. Even though what she'd seen of the Chamber of Commerce office led Lindsay to believe it would be a casual, relaxed atmosphere, she'd still wanted to make a good impression on her first day. She'd chosen a blush-pink sweater with a sweetheart neckline, a gray knee-length pencil skirt with a small ruffle at the hem and a matching pair of suede pumps.

She could walk for miles in the shoes, but the skirt's narrow fit made matching her boss's hurried strides a challenge. "Patricia…"

The other woman didn't slow down as they walked along Main Street. Most of the businesses had their doors propped open to invite the summer breeze and summer tourists inside. Many had decorated the storefront windows in themes of red, white and blue for the upcoming holiday, a palette of colors that extended to the ruffled petunias crowding the brick planters along the sidewalk.

"We're almost there."

There, as it turned out, was the square at the center of town—a lush tree-lined park where almost all the major events in town took place. A small crowd had already gathered at the white lattice gazebo near the front of the park. Two bouquets of pink and white balloons tied to the railings on the sides of the steps swayed in the cool early-morning air, as did the banner stretched across the front of the small structure.

Lindsay stumbled, and it wasn't her skirt or her shoes slowing her footsteps, but the words on the banner that brought her to a sudden stop. The words and the man standing beneath the sign.

Frozen in place some five yards away, Lindsay sucked in a quick breath as other details slowly sank in. Ryder's family standing off to one side of the gazebo; Robbie and her grandmother on the other side, huge grins lighting both of their faces. Excited whispers and the creak of the wood as Ryder's foot hit the first step. The warmth in his gaze as his measured stride erased the distance between them.

"Ryder, what is all this?" she asked, surprised she could hear the sound of her own voice over the pulse pounding in her ears.

Dappled sunlight glinted on the golden streaks in his brown hair, and the breeze rippled his white button-down shirt across his chest. His smile teased her as he reached up to cup her face in his hands. Hands that trembled ever so slightly against her flushed skin. "You've always liked to read, Lindsay. I kinda thought the sign said it all."

The sign...and the big, bold capital letters that spelled out the words *I love you, Lindsay.*

"But in case seeing isn't believing..." His chest expanded on a breath as he announced, "I love you, Lindsay. I've waited far too long to tell you, and that's why I wanted to say it here and now. I couldn't believe how lucky I was to get a second chance when you came back to town, and that was before you told me Robbie was my son. And that...that changed everything."

"I know, and I'm sorry I—"

"No, don't! Don't be sorry. Don't be anything but proud of the amazing job you've done in raising our son. I blamed you for keeping him away when I should have thanked you for bringing him back. For coming back into my life. You and Robbie are the best things to have ever happened to me."

"I didn't think you'd ever trust me again...ever love me."

"It wasn't you, sweetheart. I was afraid to trust myself. I'd already hurt you once, and with so much at stake, I told myself it would be better if I kept my distance. But the truth is, there's too much at stake for me not to take a chance. To have you and Robbie in my life, for the three of us to be a family, that's worth any risk, and I swear to you, Lindsay, I am not going to blow it this time."

"Come on, Mom!" Barely restrained energy had Robbie bouncing on his toes as he called out, "You're supposed to say yes!"

Lindsay gazed up into Ryder's eyes, seeing the love, the hope, the promise... "Say yes?" she echoed. "I don't remembering hearing a question."

"You always were a stickler for details." But despite the

complaint, Ryder slid his palms down her shoulders and took her hands in his own as he dropped to one knee. A soft gasp sounded from the group gathered behind them as he asked, "Lindsay Brookes, will you marry me?"

"This is the part," she answered her son softly without taking her gaze from the love she saw shining in Ryder's eyes, "where I say yes. Yes, I love you. Yes, I'll marry you."

Robbie mimicked her acceptance with his own exuberant response as Ryder rose to his feet and pulled Lindsay into his arms and kissed her in front of everyone...

One of the balloons broke free of its tethering ribbon, drifting toward the blue sky overhead, and Lindsay thought her heart would go sailing right alongside the bright, bobbing balloon. Because after ten years of waiting, all of Clearville finally knew that she was Ryder Kincaid's girl.

* * * * *

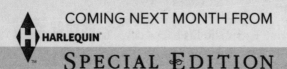

COMING NEXT MONTH FROM

HARLEQUIN

SPECIAL EDITION

Available April 21, 2015

#2401 NOT QUITE MARRIED
The Bravos of Justice Creek • by Christine Rimmer
After a fling with Dalton Ames on an idyllic island, Clara Bravo wound up pregnant. She never told Dalton the truth, since the recently divorced hunk insisted he wasn't interested in a relationship. But when Dalton discovers Clara's secret, he's determined to create a forever-after with the Bravo beauty and their baby...no matter how much she protests!

#2402 MY FAIR FORTUNE
The Fortunes of Texas: Cowboy Country
by Nancy Robards Thompson
On the outside, PR guru Brodie Fortune Hayes is the perfect British gentleman. But on the inside, he's not as polished as he seems. When Brodie is hired to fix up the image of Horseback Hollow's Cowboy Country theme park, one lovely Texan—his former fling Caitlyn Moore—might just be the woman who can open his heart after all!

#2403 A FOREVER KIND OF FAMILY
Those Engaging Garretts! • by Brenda Harlen
Daddy. That's one role Ryan Garrett never thought he'd occupy...until his friend's death left him with custody of a fourteen-month-old. He definitely didn't count on gorgeous Harper Ross stepping in to help with little Oliver. As they butt heads and sparks fly, another Garrett bachelor finds the love of a lifetime!

#2404 FOLLOWING DOCTOR'S ORDERS
Texas Rescue • by Caro Carson
Dr. Brooke Brown has devoted her entire life to her career—but that doesn't mean she isn't susceptible to playboy firefighter Zach Bishop's smoldering good looks. A fling soon turns into so much more, but Brooke's tragic past and Zach's newly discovered future might stand in the way of the family they've always wanted.

#2405 FROM BEST FRIEND TO BRIDE
The St. Johns of Stonerock • by Jules Bennett
Police chief Cameron St. John has always loved his best friend, Megan Richards—and not just in a platonic way. But there's too much baggage for friendship to turn into romance, so Cameron sets his feelings aside...until Megan's life is threatened by her dangerous brother. Then Cameron will stop at nothing to protect her—and ensure their future together.

#2406 HIS PREGNANT TEXAS SWEETHEART
Peach Leaf, Texas • by Amy Woods
Katie Bloom has fallen on hard times. She's pregnant and alone, and the museum where she works is going out of business. Now Ryan Ford, the one who got away, walks into a local eatery, tempting her with his soulful good looks. Ryan's got secrets, but can he put Katie and her child above everything else to create a lifelong love?

HSECNM0415

REQUEST YOUR FREE BOOKS!
2 FREE NOVELS PLUS 2 FREE GIFTS!

♦ HARLEQUIN

SPECIAL EDITION
Life, Love & Family

SPECIAL EXCERPT FROM

 HARLEQUIN

SPECIAL EDITION

*Harper Ross and Ryan Garrett are joint guardians for
their best friends' baby...but the heat between them is
undeniable. Can passion turn to love...and create the
family they both long for?*

Read on for a sneak preview of
A FOREVER KIND OF FAMILY,
the latest installment in **Brenda Harlen***'s*
THOSE ENGAGING GARRETTS! *miniseries.*

When Harper had gone back to work a few days after
the funeral, Ryan had offered to be the one to get up in
the night with Oliver so that she could sleep through. It
wasn't his fault that she heard every sound that emanated
from Oliver's room, across the hall from her own.

Thankfully, she worked behind the scenes at *Coffee
Time with Caroline*, Charisma's most popular morning
news show, so the dark circles under her eyes weren't as
much a problem as the fog that seemed to have enveloped
her brain. And that fog was definitely a problem.

"Do you want me to get him a drink?" she asked as
Ryan zipped up Oliver's sleeper.

"I can manage," he assured her. "Go get some sleep."

Just as she decided that she would, Oliver—now clean
and dry—stretched his arms out toward her. "Up."

Ryan deftly scooped him up in one arm. "I've got you,
buddy."

The little boy shook his head, reaching for Harper.

"Up."

"Harper has to go night-night, just like you," Ryan said.

"*Up,*" Oliver insisted.

Ryan looked at her questioningly.

She shrugged. "I've got breasts."

She'd spoken automatically, her brain apparently stuck somewhere between asleep and awake, without regard to whom she was addressing or how he might respond.

Of course, his response was predictably male—his gaze dropped to her chest and his lips curved in a slow and sexy smile. "Yeah—I'm aware of that."

Her cheeks burned as her traitorous nipples tightened beneath the thin cotton of her ribbed tank top in response to his perusal, practically begging for his attention. She lifted her arms to reach for the baby, and to cover up her breasts. "I only meant that he prefers a softer chest to snuggle against."

"Can't blame him for that," Ryan agreed, transferring the little boy to her.

Oliver immediately dropped his head onto her shoulder and dipped a hand down the front of her top to rest on the slope of her breast.

"The kid's got some slick moves," Ryan noted.

Harper felt her cheeks burning again as she moved over to the chair and settled in to rock the baby.

Fall in love with A FOREVER KIND OF FAMILY by Brenda Harlen, available May 2015 wherever Harlequin® Special Edition books and ebooks are sold.

www.Harlequin.com

HARLEQUIN®
A Romance FOR EVERY MOOD™

Love the Harlequin book you just read?

Your opinion matters.

Review this book on your favorite book site, review site, blog or your own social media properties and share your opinion with other readers!

Be sure to connect with us at:
Harlequin.com/Newsletters
Facebook.com/HarlequinBooks
Twitter.com/HarlequinBooks

HREVIEWS

JUST CAN'T GET ENOUGH?

Join our social communities
and talk to us online.

You will have access to the latest
news on upcoming titles and special
promotions, but most importantly,
you can talk to other fans about your
favorite Harlequin reads.

Harlequin.com/Community

Facebook.com/HarlequinBooks

Twitter.com/HarlequinBooks

Pinterest.com/HarlequinBooks